"Elizabeth Mavor relishes spirited, unorthodox women, free with their tongues and ready to snap their fingers at convention."

—Janet Adam Smith, *London Review of Books*

"A study of love, considered in turn as companionship, sickness and mystic devotion . . . a book whose unusual infatuations are well worth lingering over, and puzzling out."

—Russell Davies, *The Observer*

"Elizabeth Mavor is a *précieuse* without being *ridicule*. Her dialogue is stylized and stylish, but the note once pitched is skillfully stuck to. Her plot is formal, unfolded with a measured, steady hand. Symbols recognizably smile or frown at you as you go along, like statuettes bordering a cossetted flower-garden. The whole book is very much of a 'performance,' at once graceful, mannered and, in no pejorative sense, remote."

—David Williams, *The Times*

"Buoyant and witty . . . full of English idiosyncrasy and of English nonsense and intelligence."

—Karl Miller

"A thoughtful, intensely lyrical book."

—Roger Garfitt, *The Listener*

A GREEN EQUINOX

A GREEN EQUINOX

ELIZABETH MAVOR

McNally Editions

New York

McNally Editions
134 Prince St.
New York, NY 10012

Copyright © 1973 by Elizabeth Mavor
All rights reserved
Printed in the United States of America
Originally published in 1973 by Michael Joseph, Ltd.
and Wildwood House, London.
First McNally Editions paperback, 2023

ISBN: 978-1-946022-68-4
E-book: 978-1-946022-69-1

Designed by Jonathan Lippincott

3   5   7   9   10   8   6   4   2

'What you do
Still betters what is done.
. . . when you do dance, I wish you
A wave o' the sea, that you might ever do
Nothing but that; move still, still so,
And own no other function.'

The Winter's Tale

'No white nor red was ever seen
So am'rous as this lovely green.'

Andrew Marvell,
'The Garden'

'. . . the art of being miserable for misery's sake, has been brought to great perfection in our days; and the ancient Odyssey, which held forth a shining example of the endurance of real misfortune, will give place to a modern one, setting out a more instructive picture of querulous impatience under imaginary evils.'

Mr Flosky from Thomas Love Peacock,
Nightmare Abbey

The author is grateful to Thames and Hudson Ltd for permission to quote from *From Rococo to Revolution* by Michael Levey on page 139; and to Routledge and Kegan Paul Ltd for permission to quote four lines from 'Sonnet in Memory of the Lady Elizabeth Hastings' from *The Collected Poems of Sidney Keyes,* edited by M. Meyer, on page 199.

A GREEN EQUINOX

ONE

Last night while you were asleep I lay awake beside you planning your epitaph. I saw the words in Gill chiselled into the stone of the urn containing your ashes, and beside the urn, pouring its leaves over you, a willow. In a sort of pleasurable grief I tried out the various possibilities; first high Italian sentiments, then French, then Latin ('non sum, non fui, non curo' halted me for a moment; I like that. 'I am not, I was not, I care not'), then I moved on to the little Greek I know. I rejected this, however, because no one would understand it nowadays, and I'd want them to know what you've been to me. I also experimented in the phrases, convoluted as broccoli, of Sir Thomas Browne, and in the neat unexcitable periods of Pope, and finally I tried to compose in the bloodless contemporary jargon in which you and I have to speak to one another, my own love. You who are not yet dead.

It was an indulgence I enjoyed. You would have despised it, for much as you love trees you'd object to the willow, and the urn would only make you laugh. I remember quite well how you mocked just such an urn with your walking-stick in a Welsh graveyard: a vast, breasty, buttocky pot it was, teetering on an inadequate stone stalk and swollen like a pink granite womb with the romantic bones of some Georgian parson's wife who insisted on direct descent from Cadwallader. It only served to show, you said at the time, what a fatuous attitude people have towards death.

Death. At that point I gave up writing epitaphs and lay back beside you, and while I waited for sleep I retraced the road which brought me to you. Unbelievably it took only six months, equinox to equinox.

It had its starting-point late on a March afternoon at the end of a still, mizzling day. There were four people in the shop cropping along the shelves, and I was turning over the pages of a broken-backed book of early flower portraits, unable to make up my mind whether to break it up for prints or to take the trouble of repacking it. To destroy it or not, but I love what is old. I should explain straight away that I have the Great Sickness. No, not that particular sickness, though there have been moments in my life of such amorous idiocy that I probably deserved even that. No, I allude to that far worse sickness for those afflicted with it, that passion, that love affair, sexual almost, with the lost past. Friends have, of course, tried to persuade me that if such a passion is not a sickness then it's a sin, like hubris or tristitia or worst of all accidie, that devilish torpor, that restless sadness, which of all of them perhaps most nearly resembles what I suffer from, and they have advised me to stop squandering my vivacity and intelligence and, instead, discipline myself by bringing up a child, or doing social work. I, however, have read Freud carefully, and I think differently, and I know that it's not sin but a sickness, with symptoms.

Of course there's something wrong, some imbalance, or why else should I gorge myself on second-hand books of history and travel and topography, even on old floras, seeking a world that I can now never, never inhabit. I remember one book particularly, *Reckitt's Guide to East Anglia* I think it is, which tells you how nowadays (c. 1911) you can hire a wherry that can sleep eight and has a crew of two and a grand piano, all that for just three guineas a week. You can get there direct from King's Cross and buy a luncheon basket at the station with cups and knives and spoons and glasses, chicken, hot bread rolls, mustard, apple pie and a bottle of Beaujolais for 3/6 a head. Then not long ago I found Trimmer's 1869 *Flora of Middlesex*, and I read there that 'the Meadow Orchis is abundant!' round Pinner; that 'it is plentiful!' in a meadow near Hendon; and that the rare *Viola palustris* is still flourishing behind Jack Straw's Castle on Hampstead Heath. There is a pencil note in the margin at this point which says, 'Still there 1892. Wood-Smith'. 'Still there . . .' How can I express the sweet anguish aroused by those doomed words, 'Still there . . .'?

The shop door swung open and someone came in, closing it carefully behind them. For a moment I didn't look up because I was so deep in my moral debate as to whether or not I should destroy that book of prints. Eventually I laid it aside and raised my eyes. They were trapped instantly and held, by those eyes, blue and water-clear, of the Enemy.

For a moment only I was appalled. Yet it was just such a confrontation that I'd feared for two long years now, though as time went on I'd become accustomed to fearing,

the keenness of my alarm diminished perhaps by so frequently seeing her shopping or motoring through Beaudesert with her children. Soon, and shamefully, because
it almost always does, the appalled feeling began to give
way to one of amusement, for to be fair it was not she but
I who was really the Enemy though she wasn't to know it.

Now, did this sort of thing concern me? Did I think I
could be interested? she was asking me. She had, as I would
have expected, the usual rather belling upper-class voice,
the kind of voice one knew she'd have by merely looking
at her. Concerned, as it happened, I was not, for very good
reasons that I would be prepared to give, though I didn't
say so then. Interested, of course, though not in what she
seemed to be talking about (Race Relations, Pollution,
H-bombs, perhaps even Noise Abatement). In her, however, I was interested. I was face to face after all with the
woman who could destroy my peace.

Hughie hardly ever spoke of her, partly because he was
too good-mannered, partly because I think he thought
I'd be jealous. When he did speak of her it was always
and deliberately with affection. Theirs was an old marriage to ponder, for it seemed that, while he quite genuinely loved her, he was at the same time dreadfully bored
with her. Belle was Catholic. Unfortunately she was not
only a convert but an avant-garde one, which was very bad
luck for Hugh, who would so much have enjoyed meeting
Establishment Catholics, people like monseigneurs and
wonderful reactionary old bishops who like you to kiss
their rings. As it was Belle appeared to be absorbed in the
secularisation of practically everything that was in any
way arcane or ritualistic, and regularly attended gatherings

in already secularised country houses to achieve this end,
something that could in no way appeal to Hugh.

Looking at her in those first short moments I thought,
Oh yes I know you! Oh yes! An external, a useful, an
uncomplicated, a clearly-charted life. Here, I knew, was
somebody who believed in planning, in the future, in
the dignity of man. O Holy Britomart! She was fair, big-
breasted and scrubbed. Nordic. What virtuous nourish-
ment would ooze obligingly from those globular breasts.
Mine were trim and neat and rakish, because they'd been
used only for making love and not feeding children. Their
aureoles were turkey brown as befitted an adventuress,
while hers, I knew, for all that they should have gone
brown bearing children, would still have the sucked pink
look of uninterfered-with virginity.

'As you can see, this sort of thing—it's mainly a question of publicity,' she was saying. She spoke extremely
clearly, in a voice which was like flawless bronze, softly
gonged. 'On the whole people seem pretty keen,' she said.

I bet, I thought with cooling heart, for ours is a keen
little town composed as it is almost entirely of one class,
the intelligent if not always cultivated middle. This is due
to the Chemical Weapons Establishment nearby which
succeeded the gravel workings which once provided Beaudesert's livelihood. These were discontinued some time ago
leaving ravaged meadows eaten out with water-swamped
fistulas and pits upon which the keen chemists sail Fireflies
in the summer, and where, in winter, they watch widgeon
through expensive Ross binoculars.

I am sorry that Aristotle in the *Politics* was not more
specific about the desirable proportions of class and

occupation within a community. It does seem so very important to get it right, for while a preponderance of what are now called 'manual' workers seems to produce a dispiriting sameness, only occasionally spiced by that degree of eccentricity (gnomes, grots, parterres, gig wheels) which the local authority permits, too much of 'non-manual' is almost worse, just as enervating, producing such a sense of non-movement, of petrifaction. Although I own a bookshop and shamelessly live off the cultural aspirations of the inhabitants of Beaudesert, although one part of me does want to rescue what is left of the charmed past, I am nevertheless dispirited by those too perfect Georgian streets so assiduously protected by weapon-dons on the C.P.R.E., and this also goes for the careful street-lighting and the all too consciously pleasant car-free shopping precinct.

Hughie, who beneath his teasing exterior is just as wolfish an enemy of the times as I am, is constantly rubbing it in that I'm really a monster of destructiveness, that I would actually prefer all that is left now to fall into a picturesque decay rather than that the beautiful ancient, which I adore, and which I believe can only be the inheritance of the Few, and of those Few, only the very Few, should be dolled up and given a face-lift for the benefit of the disgusting Many.

He has really no right to talk like this, having shut himself away from all hurt and disappointment in the fastness of Beaudesert Park, appointed guardian, by a wealthy and discriminating Trust, of the sacred flame of culture which flickers fitfully inside what, to my way of thinking, is one of the most hideous and lowering buildings in the country. It arose, the fruit, one can only guess, of penal labour, late in the sixties of the last century, in the chateau style, and upon the ruins of something far older and, one trusts, more beautiful.

The original Beaudesert Park through the preceding centuries had been added to, partially pulled down, rebuilt, renovated, modernised and finally burnt to the ground by a pyromaniac stable-boy, leaving only its great name, its escutcheoned entrance gates, and the remains of grounds in the Kent manner protected from the advance of the despoiling gravel operations by ha-has.

The Park does house, however, protected by extremely savage alsatians, bells, tripwires and ex-Guards sergeants, a splendid collection of Louis Quinze furniture, paintings and books.

It was through books, beautiful but so dangerous books, that I first met Hugh.

'It would be exceedingly kind if you really would,' Belle Shafto was saying now. This was her expressing gratitude for my agreeing to put a notice of her (protest?) meeting in my shop window. I hadn't realised until now that she had a small child with her (there were two self-possessed older ones away at what were bound to be progressive schools). This one was very small and self-possessed and of uncertain sex owing to warm clothing. A barricade of old copies of the *Illustrated London News* had concealed its activities from view until now. It was engaged in caressing the yielding cream belly of the shop cat, and when it suddenly looked up I saw that it had Hughie's golden eyes, which made me feel oddly, not because I have ever wanted children for I haven't, but because those quiet gold eyes were windows into a room, one that I, the mistress of my love, with my timed secrecy, my fruitless pleasure, was shut out from. I knew, who doesn't, the chaos of crying and wetness and anxiety, the deadly tiredness that pervades such rooms, but at that moment I also glimpsed something else, an unfamiliar and rather loving dimension of sex, private rather than secret, gentle rather than passionate. Also tender, singing, comfortable, a room where in mutual tolerance past and present and future were seamlessly knitted up. It may only have been the interest that a childless woman sometimes has in the woman with children, or again it may have been the perennial and mutual fascination that the wife holds for the mistress, the mistress for the wife; but whichever it was I turned back to Belle and found her for the first time mysterious, almost intriguing.

'I don't suppose,' she was asking with her frank gaze, and she smiled, cleanly and whitely, in a way that was snow and sharp-cut fir trees, whilst I by comparison was a messy Neapolitan back street, 'I don't suppose that by any chance you'd like to come to our meeting?' I honestly didn't know what it was I was being asked to (Unmarried mothers? Dangerous toys? Abortion? Pink-foot geese? There are new ones every day); it could have been anything, but curiosity, also amusement, also, I realise now, a desire both sweet and wicked to tempt fate, made me say quite uncharacteristically, Yes!

After she'd gone I found myself wondering whether Hughie would laugh about this or be angry. We had agreed long ago that his wife and I were bound to meet some time or other, living as we did in such a small town, she a semi-public woman because she was married to the gauleiter of Beaudesert Park, and I semi-public too because of owning the only bookshop in the place. Actually it was amazing that we hadn't met before. What Hugh would say at once, of course, was that although our meeting had always been likely, probably inevitable, I needn't have immediately committed myself on Belle's account to an occasion concerned with something (Nuclear tests? Gay Lib? Dyslexia?) in which I had not the slightest interest. Why in God's name had I done it? I am not afraid of Hugh, but I do love him I think. In the end I'd probably turn chicken and cancel the whole thing. I hadn't, after all, actually promised to go. So for a time I dismissed it from my mind.

Until now Hughie's and my assignations had been hardly deserving of so colourful a name. They were simple and easy to effect. The library at Beaudesert was not only an antiquarian but also a working library used by scholars, and it was in need of regular attention, the kind of attention my small but specialised business is so very well qualified to give. Not only do we provide the leather restorative (an acidless receipt given to me by an old Florentine collector) but I also repair and bind the books myself. Long ago that passion which I have for the beautiful ancient led me to learn bookbinding, and since then I have not only equipped myself with all the necessary tools of my craft, but I have also one of the finest collections of antique fleurons in the country. I began acquiring them some years ago when all the other binders, seeing no further use for them, were throwing them out by the boxful—all the minute urns and willows and suns and roses and fish and harps which in gold had embellished the leather spines of eighteenth-century books.

Hughie, like me, also collects, but in the more esoteric seventeenth century, thus communication between us is not only an affair of great pleasure but of enjoyable business. Belle, I had always understood, while admiring and encouraging Hugh's interest, has, as one might guess, little use herself for the fine page or the beautiful binding. The books that she consults are honest, unpampered creatures which have to work. Paperbacks.

Hugh did in fact come that night. There was a volume of Shenstone that needed re-backing. He came by the side door, because by then I'd closed the shop and withdrawn into my eyrie above, where I have a small flat with the usual offices and a pleasant parlour-like room lined with the best books.

It was to be an off night. Hughie had already eaten, and I had nothing suitable to drink on top of one of Belle's pilaffs, which were apt to be distending. In addition he was in a state of siege neurosis having just had a letter from some kind of educational organisation demanding, literally demanding, a five-day residential course in May on eighteenth-century books and furniture. Because of this, but also, looking back, because of some instinctive disinclination of my own, I put off telling him about the day's meeting with Belle.

It was to be an off night when we lay together too. Perfunctory. This had already happened sufficiently recently to make me unhappy, despairing momentarily, as one does, of ever having again the marvellous and secret honey which we had once shared together. He could be a precious lover, and, unlike the others, could recreate from my body, neat, self-contained and selfish as in the beginning I think it was, a landscape from Paradise. One in whose leaves and secret rills and trembling sunlight we had laughed and bathed together, ravished.

'Oh God! Oh God! Oh God!' he cried when it was over.

'What on earth's the matter?'

'Five bleeding appalling days!' He described them, beating the air with his neat legs. Each one of them would be a triple crucifixion. How he hated everything now! How he had got to hate culture itself, which was after all his bread and butter. Cried out how he loathed all their beastly expressions, the Rewarding, the Enriching, the Meaningfulness. 'But the Feeling!' he yelled. 'The Feeling!'

'Kiss me again,' I said, 'and then you can tell me about it.'

'Surgery! Concept! Probe!' he replied, ungratefully. 'Bottleneck!'

'Dialogue!' I said, stroking him.

'Skills!'

'Skills came in,' I said, 'and Skill went out!'

'I love you!' he suddenly said and laughed.

'Not actually my joke,' I said. 'An old sour one by now!'

'I know it is, but I still love you!'

'Only because I pander so slavishly to your deathly meanness, your prejudice, your backward-staring.'

'You listen to me! You take my word for it! It's later than you think up here in Joyous Garde. They're only waiting to mine a great breach in the outer walls and then they'll all pour in and plaster their filthy hands all over the sacred treasure of the ages.'

'You might say they'll plaster their sacred hands over the filthy treasure of the ages,' I said, 'and anyhow, who are "They"?' I interlaced my fingers with his.

'"They" are not "Us." We are the last of the truly lovely people,' he said and lit a complacent cigarette.

'Actually we're not lovely at all,' I said, though as a matter of fact he was lovely. 'We are arrogant and overprivileged.'

'That's what I call lovely nowadays.'

'We are mean and splenetic and selfish; indeed we are dross.'

'Dross? Dross? O lovely, lovely Dross!' and he kissed me again. 'Think of them all in their working-parties and workshops, all their sit-ins, pray-ups, fall-outs, and all they're actually doing is colonising. If only they could see themselves for what they really are, the New Imperialists. That's where all the energy of the country's going, in Aunt-Edna-like Imperialism! So thank God, thank God, for the Dross!'

'Well, well, what is it you believe then?' I asked, and entangled his long hair gently in my fingers. Such fine silky hair, and he had long lashes, and a long thin mouth which, when he was going to laugh, puckered viciously at the corners as though he'd just sucked a lemon.

'I believe in Michaelangelo,' he began, dreamily closing his eyes, 'in Velasquez and Rembrandt; in the might of design, the mystery of colour, the redemption of all things by Beauty everlasting'—what great stuff! 'But oh!' he cried opening his gold eyes, 'if only I did! No, you must ask me something much more interesting. Please ask me what I don't believe in!'

'Precious love, what don't you believe in?' I had of course heard it all before.

Certainly not in the dignity of man, nor in man's rights, nor in man's bottomless capacity for improvement, nor yet in man's natural goodness, which is ascribed to his human heart. Above all the heart must not be believed. It was perhaps the heart he dreaded more than anything. The sleep of reason produced monsters. He was terrified of the feeling heart.

'All the words they use!' he cried sitting up. 'Every one of them a great kick on the scrotum!'

Disturbed! Handicapped! Unacademic! Disorientated! As though what was criminal, mad, stupid and cruel, had been eliminated from the world by the mere use of these words and the millennium come at last, which it hadn't.

'Say just that then,' I said, 'say that at your five days' wonder.'

'And Belle's such a sucker for all these words,' he said moodily. 'She uses them constantly; it really gets on one's wick.'

'Well?'

'Well, I'll think about it. About how to say it I mean. Poor Belle!' he added.

It occurred to me then that it would be even more difficult now for me to tell him about my meeting with his wife and the subsequent rendezvous we had planned.

'But O lovely! O wild! O secret! O dark, dark barbarian! My ambiguous Hero!'

'Romantic fool!'

'So wilful, so mad and bad and dangerous to know!'

I could have loved him again then, and I dare say it would have been much better than before. I am a little like Madame de Warens, who was able at any time to interrupt a discussion on art or whatever to make love, and then could resume the interrupted discussion immediately

15

afterwards as though nothing had happened. Hugh, alas, was not like this. The unpleasing euphemisms we had been discussing had upset him, and he went. He left me alone in our white crumpled bed listening to the fine rain of the spring night flying like scattered poppy seeds against the window.

I lay still for some time after the door had closed and then, too restless to sleep, I got up and went downstairs into the dark shop where Belle's notice was still lying on the counter. It turned out to be all I had feared. Waiting to spring like some disagreeable jungle creature from its liana-like forest of jargon, was an invitation to meet, in order to love, over tea or coffee, one's neighbour.

TWO

Hugh Shafto walked slowly along the flowered silk length of the Blue Gallery. The spring sunlight struck through great windows, which happily excluded the east wind that scoured the gardens outside, and pleasantly warmed his cheek and neck. He had been warmed too by Belle's good coffee and by the friendly but deferential greetings of his ex-Guards N.C.O.s in the hall below. To crown this well-fledged morning there was waiting in his office, he knew, a case of French eighteenth-century books to be gone over. It was a gift from one of the Trust's well-wishers and contained among other delights, so the list said, a large paper edition of the *Nouvelle Héloïse* with Gravelot engravings. Hero must see those, he thought, they would be very much to her taste, she would love them. Future delights with the books, the whole benevolence of the morning, had momentarily succeeded in reducing the unpleasing prospect of that event which loomed in May. Let it wait! One had to be philosophical, and whatever horror was in store, and he had no doubt that there were horrors in store, he was captain of his castle for this morning anyway. Guard had been inspected, security checked, and now he was moving through the two great rooms which housed the world-famous collection of Sèvres. It was a collection so hideously valuable that the lady custodians of Beaudesert had been instructed that, suppose they and a piece of Sèvres should one day find themselves together upon a ladder, and one or other being unhappily forced to drop and break, it must regrettably be the human leg, not the Sèvres.

He walked, not as other men and women must, who have the lady custodians snapping at their heels and who will encounter electric booby traps should they wish to examine anything closely, but in the manner of the seigneurs for whom, after all, such beauty was first made. Hugh was free any time, provided an ex-Guards N.C.O. was there to protect him, to unlock a case, and take out some precious thing, a parrot, a tureen, a snuffbox, and hold it, lovingly, in his hand.

Apart from his very real appreciation of the beautiful, Hugh's, and this was no doubt why the Trust had chosen him, was the perfect siege mentality. It was a mentality that some might unkindly have called rather womanish, doting on its confines to the point of flaccidity, only showing its real strength under attack and insult. It was only then that one saw passion, saw a creature convinced of the absolute and priceless rectitude of its standards for which it was prepared to die. The perils of such a psychology are unspeakable, and are only just balanced by its great compensation which is, when aroused, a vivid sense of purpose. The final reward for such thinking is, of course, death, but also immortality. To see Hugh in a rage was to be put in mind of extravagances like the fall of Carthage, the rape of Lucrece, the taking of Constantinople . . .

I am a well-balanced man, he was thinking as he made for his office where the *Nouvelle Héloïse* and Rosa, his secretary, awaited him. In this opinion he was including not only his own nature, which he knew did have its weak spots, but his fortunate exterior circumstances—his idealistic wife, his cynic mistress, both of whom adored him. He had never felt the force of those charming lines from the *Beggar's Opera*, which he nevertheless sometimes sang to Hero after making love to her:

> How happy could I be with either
> Were t'other dear charmer away . . .

Rather he felt that one charmer lent even further charm to the other, each unknowingly conspiring in a sort of dialectic to make him, had the world been a less repulsive place than it was, the happiest and kindest of men.

He reached the door of his office which was ajar and called cheerfully to Rosa King's bottom. The rest of her was lowered into what must certainly be his treasured box of books.

'How is Madame Rosa this morning?'

She succeeded in keeping some sort of order in the office, though only just, tending to be over-enthusiastic as well as over-sensitive. She was probably too intelligent to be a really good secretary. Her wishes were not, as they should have been, always his.

'Lovely, lovely books! Yum, yum!' she said straightening, her beautiful dark eyes guttering with barely contained brightness. Hugh saw with annoyance and a disappointment which he knew was childish, that she had broached the precious case, unasked.

'Look! Look!' Morocco sumptuously gilded.

He resisted the desire to say 'Put it down, Rosa!' It sounded too like a dog; besides she was subject to frightening pets if corrected, and to Hugh's alarm would move heavily about the office breathing deeply through her nostrils and banging things until her daemonic energy was discharged and a sort of calm achieved. This usually took some time. He didn't want anything like that this morning as he had a great deal of correspondence to get through, so he simply said 'Mmm!' which was cowardly, and picked up the field-glasses which he kept on his desk in case there were any interesting birds about on the lawns. He raised them to his eyes and began slowly sweeping them over the expanse of garden framed by the window.

They moved past the architrave, the quartz in its hideous alien stone winking blindly in the sunlight, moved smoothly through the swelling copper buds of a nearby beech tree, then down its green trunk to the parterre below where they trapped, beside an inane-looking stone Melpomene with a ruffled-looking robin perched on her shoulder, a gardener raking gravel. And from the gardener he swept the glasses up again and, freer, far freer than the robin, he trained them along the great vista which led east and which was bounded on either side by twin canals stone-edged, which converged at a point just below the rising morning sun and between skilfully positioned plantings of beech and larch.

By now he knew that Rosa had registered his meek protest. He could feel her, book still in hand, looking at him. 'Let her suffer,' he thought cheerfully, and swung the glasses to the left, moving swiftly over the larches and down along a copse of sweet chestnut until, tracking the course of a ring-dove flying with each feather marvellously defined, he dipped with the dove into a clearing in the boskage where could be glimpsed the fiery sparkle of water. Beside it was the farmhouse where his mother lived.

'How is Mrs Shafto?' Rosa asked instantly.

'Oh, I don't know. All right, I think.'

He could see smoke rising from the farmhouse, blowing whispily hither and thither, and down by the edge of the blazing mirror of water he could see someone moving.

'She's an extraordinarily interesting woman, your mother!' Rosa said.

'Do you think so?' he asked tiredly, then smiled and lowered the glasses, forgiving her. There were aeons of defensive history at the back of this question.

'Are we ready then?' demanded Rosa with that mixture of impertinence and expedition which she reserved for such occasions. He noticed, however, that she had returned the book to its box.

Down at the water's edge Mrs Shafto in waders and anorak was adjusting the hectically flapping sail of a large model clipper. From time to time she exclaimed quietly to herself. On the bank a black pug, its protuberant eyes blinking against the drying wind, sat watching her gravely.

'Oh damn!' cried Mrs Shafto, fiddling with tiny cords. Around her the snaking river wavelets lapped away from her bulk in incessant concentric rings, out and out to break softly upon the shallow beaches of the miniature islands which Mrs Shafto had skilfully planted with wild cherry and nut trees, and where, in spring, encouraged by Mrs Shafto, Lent lilies, wood anemones and violets blew and multiplied.

The small farmhouse which stood on the very brink of the water had been neglected and windowless when Kate Shafto had first found it. Once a neat and compact meadowland farm, the land had been sold in the late twenties to speculators, and gravel-workings had grouched and flooded away its substance. Kate Shafto had bought the watery waste ten years ago for what was then termed a song.

She had seen its possibilities instantly. Standing there in driving rain and beneath the tearing lavender clouds of an autumn afternoon, she had gazed through and beyond the melancholy heaps of curry-coloured subsoil, the ponds of black and violet water that the dredgers had left behind, seeing instead a redeemed landscape with an archipelago, ports for her sailing-ships, a necessary haven for immigrant duck. It had been the same with the house when she and Hugh had struggled past the unhinged door and explored the dark chill rooms which stank of decaying food and excrement. To Hugh's dismay she hadn't appeared to register the ominous symptoms and tumbled bricks and plaster in the ugly fireplace, because she was seeing—how could he guess?—a bright fire burning from carefully collected sticks. She had been similarly, and to Hugh irritatingly, oblivious to the damp patches which clouded every

wall, appearing more interested in opening the unwilling
casements in the upper rooms and leaning out to exclaim
delightedly at the large yew tree which rubbed and sang
in its dark leaves against the western end of the house, its
roots without a doubt interfering seriously with the stabil-
ity of the foundations.

It had seemed a calamitous decision to Hugh when she
decided to buy the place. Calamitous not only from her
point of view, but his own. Even then he'd had hopes of
Beaudesert, was, in a manner of speaking, already in love
with and waiting for it. That his mother by her intended
purchase should canker this roseate dream before it had
even been realised seemed an act of diabolical selfishness.
He said so. She, with the air of one who has registered
but is not prepared to comment upon an unfortunate
social gaffe, ignored him. This was her calf-country after
all, despoiled perhaps, vulgarised certainly, but her own.
Widowed, she was returning to it. Eight years afterwards
Hugh succeeded to Beaudesert and came to live beside her.

With lean active fingers that belied the bulk of her
wrapped figure, Mrs Shafto tenderly slackened and ad-
justed the Lilliputian clew-lines, bunt-lines, sheets. All at
once the irritable shaking ceased, and from between her
spread fingers the ship, its sails smooth-spread and white as
the breast of a swan, glided slowly away. She straightened
to watch it, shading with her hand heavy-lidded eyes the
colour of sweet sherry, a nose high-bridged as a conquistador's, an upper lip, long and humorous, that was curling
delightedly.

'Julia!' she cried over her shoulder towards the open
garden windows of the house. 'Julia!' Her voice had a

husky catch to it that made it memorable, rather attractive. 'Julia!' The pug began to bark frenziedly, bounding comma-shaped upon the bank. 'Shut up!' cried Mrs Shafto as a woman came hurrying out through the open front door twisting her wet hands in a tea-towel. She was brown and heavily built, not unlike Mrs Shafto herself.

'Ah bravissima! Bravissima!' she screamed, filling the shocked air with salvoes and ecstatic bunting.

For the ship, cleaving sweetly through the sea to the north-west of the archipelago, a tumbled column of white water at her foot, was indeed brave, an object of strange beauty; not bird not fish, it was yet alive. A creature. A harbinger.

'There, you see!' said Mrs Shafto casting up her eyes in mock self-admiration. She turned to Julia and held out her arms laughing and, with them still outstretched waded to the shore. Fleetingly the two women embraced like plump fastidious birds.

On the further side of Mrs Shafto's Caspian her ship, which she had designed herself, and which all winter, plank by ribbon-sized plank, she had been building with absorbed and devoted care, flutteringly beached herself in the soft shallows.

'Why? Why? Why?' Rosa was demanding hotly. Her nostrils were flaring, he noticed with alarm, disclosing virile tendrils of black hair. 'We have no government aid! There's no need for us to be accommodating to such people!' She was speaking of course about the bloody non-event in May.

'It's an intrusion,' she said, 'not to say an invasion!'

'Nevertheless, it's politic at least to keep up the appearance of being democratic,' replied Hugh primly. He found his own aversion drooping and dwindling in the fiery heat of Rosa's passion.

'This is not just for anybody!' she shouted, flinging wide her arms to embrace the sun-filled office and its files, the very matrix of all Beaudesert. 'This is not for the mass!' She struck a rebelliously defiant attitude like some threatened Jugurthian princess. Really, Hugh thought, he'd have to get rid of her if she went on like this.

'Within these walls there is a flame,' she cried cupping her large breasts in brown lean hands. She now looked as though she herself had suddenly become something of infinite preciousness, a temple sacrifice perhaps. 'It is a flame sacred as the fire carried in clay pots by the old tribal grandmothers millenniums ago. It is that very fire which Prometheus stole from Heaven and hushed from the wind in the hollow of a hemlock stalk!'

'That's extremely well expressed,' commented Hugh smiling. He could feel the heat of her breath which smelt of cloves. Yet he was impressed in spite of himself, made even a little envious by her passion though it exhausted him. Rosa's life style, to use one of the detestable current phrases, was one that Hugh, in theory, admired. There was the infinite care taken with cooking for instance—no pains spared in the sieving, the seething, the marinating, the pounding that might have deterred other less energetic tyros. Rosa furthermore did not take holidays. In her system one did not take holidays, one travelled, and not in cars either, but in trains by timetable and to places that one explored on foot, with maps. She would spend hours and days walking in busy cities, seeking out the great and small works of long-dead men. With the present inhabitants of the planet she was unconcerned.

'Everything the mob touches,' Rosa whispered gesturing again, only this time towards the pullulating barbarians outside the window, 'they blight!'

Woods by a deep green river in France rose to Hugh's own mind at this point, woods weirdly festooned, as in a Rackham drawing, with campers' rubbish, paper, old stockings, other unmentionables, yet the birds, unaware, had still been singing.

'Their very gaze,' hissed Rosa fixing him with her hot tea-coloured eyes, 'actually alters the spiritual aura which surrounds a work of art, drains it. Something vital goes from it with too much looking, too much photographing, too many reproductions and coloured postcards. Hugh, you must have noticed that. Think of the Ravenna mosaics!'

'Yes, yes and I remember it happening to the Redouté roses,' he agreed, 'there they were on lamps and bathroom curtains, and table mats and God knows what else. And yes, as you say, they were destroyed.'

'Then why?' yelled Rosa banging on his desk.

'Well, mightn't there be one, just one to whom the flame really meant something?' pleaded Hugh. 'One loved, lost sheep, Rosa, brought home for us all to rejoice over?' In Rosa's presence he had an urgent desire to adopt the opposite cause. He found this maddening. It seemed to corrupt his own integrity. 'We've got to be subtle in the war against the barbarian,' he explained lamely. 'We must get to know the Enemy.'

'But I already know the Enemy,' said Rosa shaking her head and assuming a Druse-like pose. 'I already know him.'

'Then we'll seduce him!' Hugh said cunningly, for in saying this he also, as he was well aware, seduced Rosa who was inconveniently highly-sexed; 'we'll set a trap. We'll turn them around.' He began to feel slightly cheered at the prospect. 'We'll do the most uncontemporary, the most outrageous, provocative things we could do, and we'll do it with, oh! such honeyed words. We'll give them,' he said, 'a Symposium on the Rococo!' Rosa stamped.

By lunchtime Hugh knew with resigned certainty that the morning's delicate equilibrium had been irretrievably lost, and he was looking forward with a good deal of relief to Belle. The fact was that Belle's politics, Belle's earnestness, Belle's very *allemanderie,* gave him a most real sense of security.

Her views bored him, it was true, but they did produce in him a benevolence which sprang, he believed, from the true tolerance of a well-educated and impartial man. There was an additional compensation, and this was the not inconsiderable sexual interest which was stimulated by their very differing opinions. Occasionally they quarrelled, but this was merely the prelude to an enjoyable sexual interchange, a delicious and cosy making-up in the privacy of their bed when he, the wise, the undeluded man, the therefore tragic, the therefore rare and romantic man, succumbed thankfully to the gentle but competent caresses of Belle Shafto, Earth Mother.

His own mother had been a washout. As far as propitiating his ego or encouraging him, that's to say.

He supposed she'd given birth to him when she'd been too young or something of the sort, for he never remembered her having been old or staid enough for his peace of mind. She had been dashing, impulsive, quick, hot, dark, impatient. Yet, from all the welter of ambivalent feeling that she evoked in him he was actually only able to dredge up one solid complaint, and this was that somehow she had taken away all power of discovery. Her vitality and her range had been exhausting. Indeed, if the hideous myth of the many-sided man, that human polygon of arrogance and conceit, had ever been in likelihood of realisation, his mother would have been a strong female candidate. She painted, she gardened, she had hunted, played polo and she had shot. She had once played tournament golf; Sir Malcolm Campbell had taught her to drive. She wrote poetry, she played the flute, she was even good with her hands. She was so restless and clever that by the time he was sixteen he realised helplessly that there was no cleft nor corner in the great field of life, now spreading so alarmingly before him, that he felt able to make his own. She had by that time tainted everything, offering him second-hand that which she herself had pristinely enjoyed, offering him it, moreover—which enraged him—with an air as though she were conferring a personal gift. This went for everything, music and painting and flowers and travel, everything important, leaving only areas that were not of the slightest interest to him—engineering, the army, local government, the law.

Lamed at the outset by her superior energy, even the considerable beauty she had put before him had not inspired him to open new ground for himself or to live a life of his own. Instead he had had to structure his life around what already existed, conserving it, holding it against any who might want to take it from him. For him the future was without interest. He possessed the past.

And so, he pondered as he paused before the last window in the Blue Gallery and gazed over the trees to where his mother's white doves wheeled in a harebell-coloured sky, I found myself a safe castle.

His and Belle's flat took up the whole of the south tower, an adjacent corridor and four bedrooms, and this, their home, was as provoking and refreshing to him as Belle herself who had designed it. It was a revulsion from the Beaudesert Rococo, which he adored. Here all was simple, solid, stripped and pickled. There were numerous pleasant objects made of limewood, of sage-coloured rush, of oatmeal linen, of burnished steel. When he came in, Belle was removing a lasagne from the oven, and its aromatic exhalations filled, deliciously, the air.

'What was this morning like?' and she bent and kissed his hair.

'Lousy. Rosa had another tantrum. She always seems to be having the curse.'

'Ah, Rosa! I thought Rosa suited you so well?' The idea of Rosa amused her. 'The very person! The very very person!' he had crowed when Rosa had first turned up. 'Damned attractive too!', by way of warning to Belle. She had never taken any notice of the threat of Rosa's attractiveness but now couldn't resist, from the resonant depths of her clear being, taunting him with affectionate malice whenever Rosa was mentioned.

'She'll have to go if she goes on like this,' he said helping himself to the lasagne.

'Oh, no! Poor Rosa, it would kill her!'

'Well what if it does?'

'Don't be so naughty!'

He began to feel soothed. He looked up into his wife's smiling sinless eyes and said 'Shut up!' And then, 'Aren't you going to eat anything?'

'No, I've already eaten.'

'Why?'

'I've got a meeting.'

Oh fuck! he thought, I wanted her to be with me until half-past two at least, or even quarter to three.

'Damn!' he said.

'And your mother rang,' she said calmly buttoning up her coat.

'Hell!'

'Yes I know, but she wants you to go and see her about something, I forget what.'

'Where are you going anyway?' he asked meanly. She must stop taking on so much, it wasn't fair to him.

'A kind of ecumenical bunfight with a film afterwards.'

'God!' he said gloomily.

She smiled. 'But I must tell you who I've got to come,' she said. 'This may surprise even you.' She stood smiling, showing her beautiful even teeth.

'Who? Nothing could surprise me.'

'Hero Kinoull. I'm rather pleased.'

'?'

'Hero Kinoull, you know her quite well, at the bookshop, she let me put my notice up in her window. I had somehow never thought of asking her before which was stupid of me.'

'?' he bellowed like a bull in sudden fright and pain. '?'

But the door had shut and she had gone.

THREE

Why, for God's sake am I made like this? So adamantine
in theory I mean, so waxlike in practice? I ask myself this
every time. As it was, I gave up an unreasonable amount
of time trying to decide not to go to Belle's meeting. Such
meetings are not, but not, for me, who am of a contem-
plative and not an active disposition: besides they bore me
so excruciatingly. But all the time a picture of Belle kept
coming into my head. Belle was so impossibly decent, so
appallingly hopeful even (funny thought!), of me. And of
course there was guilt. Guilt about the true, and on my
side, deceitful nature of our relationship. It seemed, simple-
minded though it was, that in one way at least I could be
clear and honourable towards Belle, and that was to go
to her bloody meeting. I don't think I had ever worried
before like this about keeping an engagement. I can only
say that after haggling with myself for two days, swinging
violently now in this direction now in that, when the time
came, I went.

I left my assistant and the cat to watch the shop and
walked to Belle's meeting. It was one of those douce, but

treacherous days, inviting leaves and birds, and possibly hearts, to riot, only to rebuke them with a sharp frost in the early hours. Walking to the Methodist chapel, where the meeting was, I thought of how Hughie, when he's feeling mean, likes to tell me that my shrinking from the contemporary scene, my retirement into the past, if not exactly a pose, is nevertheless a kind of double bluff. Really, he tells me, I am simply longing to identify, to join madly and enthusiastically in the hectic dance. My decision not to do so is not an intellectual decision like his, nor yet, like his, the product of a finely tutored sensibility, or so he tells me. It is, flatly expressed, a sour grapes situation. It appears that my bourgeois education inculcated hopelessly false notions of taste and morality, and along with them the pressing need to disseminate them by leadership. By the time I was mature enough to offer them, society had developed and no longer felt in need of my mildewed fruits. In fine, my state of retreat, so far from being the romantic condition I had supposed, is really one of sulky frustration.

Beaudesert, which is in the non-conformist geological corn-brash, has a charming chapel, a real Trianon in almond stucco with cream pillars; inside the décor is all beetroot and gold. As I approached I could see from the number of cars and prams and women in hats that it was going to be a larger meeting than I'd bargained for. Belle had instructed me to meet her inside, so I pressed past the stout bulk of the Beaudesert cinema manager's wife and shortly glimpsed Belle, a valkyrie, ushering a large and talkative crowd of women to their pews. When she saw me she smiled and came pushing back through the throng.

'The meeting's been cancelled!' she said.

'What's this, then?' I asked.

'Oh, it's a meeting all right, but not the one I actually asked you to. It's changed into something different now.' She laughed apologetically. I began laughing myself both at the protean nature of Belle's meetings, also at all those unnecessary forward and backward motions I'd been making the last few days. Here I was, for nothing.

'Do stay,' said Belle, dashing back her hair from her eyes with a short chopping movement like an abbreviated salute, 'because we've just heard that they're going to cut down the Bunyan Elm!'

'What on earth can we do about that?'

'Ssh!' she said bending down and whispering into my neck. 'There's Miss Eddowes!' The pressure of the crowd behind thrust us conspiratorially together, and I could smell the clean childish smell of her hair.

'They want to bulldoze it away to make a car park,' explained Belle, 'and we've got to hold them up until we get a preservation order.'

'How shall we do that?'

'Ssh! You're just about to hear!'

By now a short elderly woman in a headscarf had climbed into the pulpit.

'Ladies! Ladies! Ladies!' cried Miss Eddowes and clapped her hands. This had an impressively emollient effect. The talking ceased.

'We all know why we're here,' said Miss Eddowes.

'I thought it was going to be a coffee morning!' someone said.

'Ssh!'

'We are here to save the Bunyan Elm!' There was clapping.

It was one of Beaudesert's ancient monuments. Miss Eddowes refreshed our memories, evoked that knotted tree, its thickened trunk carrying the heavy oedematous limbs which blazed each summer with a thick viridian leafage. Its centre had rotted away into a circular chamber where a dozen children could stand. Beneath its young branches, tradition had it, said Miss Eddowes, Beaudesert's own poet had once sat, dreamed, and possibly composed. Here there was another ripple of appreciative clapping. Even if he hadn't, the tree was still an ancient meeting-place for Beaudesert's lovers and for its senior citizens. It was a safe place for children, for dogs even. There was renewed clapping. For the people of Beaudesert it was more than a tree. It was a symbol (claps), but of what? There was a brief silence as people considered what. It was no less than a symbol of England. England as it had been (claps) and as it could and would be again (cheers). It was a symbol of courage (claps), of fortitude (claps), of a resolute resistance to everything (claps and cheers). It was a sort of Mr Churchill tree (loud cheers) though of course it also meant something particular to each one of us (a honey-like silence as people thought about this). Now it was going to be felled. (Groans of disapproval and some hissing.) And for what? For the enlargement of the civic car park (groans). The horror of the move had only just come to the notice of the Beaudesert Women's Civic Trust. It was indeed the eleventh hour. (More groans.) Yet there was a last chance (everyone brightly lifted their chins). One of the planners' men had just been about to approach the lower regions of the tree with his buzz saw when a member of the Trust had intercepted it with her leg. Fortunately he had been an exceedingly pleasant man and had agreed to wait until last-minute efforts were set in train to obtain a preservation order. But a second and much less pleasant workman had intervened at that point to insist that the act of vandalism go on. The member of the Trust had then interposed the whole of herself between the tree and the disagreeable workman who'd picked up the buzz saw. Other women, not all of them in fact Trust members, had joined the fray at this stage, encircling the tree completely. This was the situation at present. An immediate and organised picketing of the tree was now necessary until such time as the preservation order should be obtained and the tree be saved. Volunteers who were willing to establish a two-hour picketing rota were urgently needed. The upper air of the chapel was filled with a waving copse of eager hands.

Beside me I felt Belle raising hers. She did it instantly and generously. I was touched to see, however, that she was looking straight ahead, kindly freeing me, I thought, to back out should I want to. I did want to, badly. But it is difficult to be the one against the many when the many are so bent upon a cause, and, in spite of myself, I could see that this cause had its merits. Pressed against Belle by the people behind, I crawled my right arm up my ribs and then uncoiled it, like a cobra, above my head. Belle had plainly been waiting for such a gesture; she now turned as much as the crush allowed and smiled down at me. I felt trapped, but gratified.

An advance detachment was now immediately sent off to relieve the beleaguered Trust member and her friends, after which a round-the-clock rota was worked out in continental time. Miss Eddowes had once been a FANY and was of a military disposition. So it was that to my dismay I shortly found myself being appointed to the dawn shift at 0300 hours.

'Not that I think it'll be necessary,' remarked Miss Eddowes who seemed to be growing more military every moment. 'The order should have come long before then. But we must at least be prepared to guard the tree right through the night. I understand the contractor's an obdurate brute, most cunning. If we leave the tree unprotected for a second he'll have it down.'

'Let's go and see how they're getting on,' Belle said when Miss Eddowes had finished giving orders. 'You know Hugh, of course?' she asked as we walked in watery sunshine down to the Platt where the tree was. I admitted steadily that I did know Hugh, and that we did do a certain amount of business together. Yet it didn't sound as amusing to say this as it ought to have done.

'He and I are very different. Completely opposite in fact, but it seems to work.'

'As long as it does.'

'You've probably realised that he's obsessed by the past? No other tense exists.'

'You mean the future is ruined in advance?' I knew how darkening Hugh could be about that.

'How funny you should say that! Well, to be fair, not always. I think I probably talk too much about the future and everything coming right in the end. Hugh says it's wearing rose-coloured spectacles, and I'm afraid he finds it very irritating.'

Poor bloody Hugh finds that irritating, I thought. 'Perhaps it's just different forms of *angst* operating,' I said. 'Insecure people usually seem to wallow in the past. People who are crazed with guilt mess about in the future.'

'Do you really think so?'

'Oh, God! I'm dreadfully sorry. I wasn't thinking what I was saying. I'm sure it doesn't apply to you; really it can't do. I've never seen anyone more exempt from guilt!'

'No, no, it doesn't matter,' said Belle beginning to laugh. 'It's probably true!'

'What do you think he would think about this?' I asked her, partly to change the subject, partly because I was genuinely interested, out of guilt and anxiety. We were now approaching the Platt, where small groups of people were standing about. I noticed that there was a number of men clustered around the curiously prehistoric outline of an enormous mustard-coloured bulldozer.

'Oh, I think he might approve in theory,' replied Belle gravely, narrowing her eyes against the gauzy rain that had started, 'but I think he'd find the practice of it too much. Hugh's rather shy, you know. I think he'd find it too embarrassing to participate. It's like everything else—the protests against the nuclear tests, marching against the Vietnam business—he'd never do it. I don't really mind that, or his laughing, but he's really thrown his hand in; he thinks we're finished, you see. I can't help minding that. I really wouldn't want to get up in the morning if I thought like that!'

Bad, bad Hugh! I thought, but what I said was, 'Well, here's a scene from the sex war if you like!'

The Platt presented a strangely dramatic confrontation. Supported by a smiling crowd, mostly of their own sex, five well-clad women were standing with their backs to the Bunyan Elm. Two had umbrellas. As we got nearer, the bulldozer, which until now had been standing silent, suddenly violently broke wind and released a thick blue column of evil-smelling exhaust. The men who were clustered about it moved back respectfully from its shaking faecal-coloured haunches as slowly, its grab rising like an enormous priapus, it began bumping forward on great slewing wheels towards the tree.

The five women, among whom I could now recognise Miss Eddowes, who must have dashed over in her Mini; the woman who kept the shoe shop in the High Street; and the ubiquitous wife of the cinema manager, calmly laid down their umbrellas and grasped hands, forming a living fence round the tree, waiting.

Beside me Belle began to run. She ran with enormous strides, so that I, who have not run for years, found it hard to keep up.

'Hoy!' she shouted. 'You can't intimidate people like that! Hoy! It isn't fair!' And then 'Shame!' she called loudly as we dashed towards the dwindling gap between the bulldozer and the women round the tree. They were beginning to shift uneasily but were still holding their ground.

'Shame!' shouted Belle breathlessly.

'Shame! Shame! Shame!' the watching women took up angrily. 'Shame!'

'Bothering bargers!' shouted someone excitedly. 'Bathering bodgers! I mean humbugs!'

'Buggers!' added someone daringly.

'Aw, piss off!' From the further end of the kind of jousting lane formed by parallel hedges of angry women, tiny men stabbed the air crossly.

'Fuck off!'

'Piss yourself!'

'Shut up!'

'Shame!'

'Shug!'

'Shiss!'

'How dare you!'

The bulldozer's grab was now within touching distance of the obstinate women. What would they do? The driver revved vigorously once or twice, releasing clouds of fumes over their heads. There was an outburst of coughing.

'Disgusting!'

'Fiends!'

'Pissers!'

When the fumes cleared the women were to be seen still gallantly holding on. For the first time the driver of the bulldozer looked uncertain. He braked violently as if just saving the women from instant death, then he climbed out of his cab, and leapt down off the machine.

'Now then, ladies!' he said.

'Piss off!' cried one woman passionately.

'Who's boss of this lot?' the man asked.

'You can count me responsible!' cried Miss Eddowes.

'And me!'

'And me!'

'And me!'

'And all of us!'

'Then, madam, would you kindly tell these ladies to leave that tree so that I can get on with my work?'

'Brute!'

'You can't frighten us!'

'Coward!'

'Not until we get the preservation order!' screamed Miss Eddowes above the hubbub.

'Snass!'

'Pus!'

'Prick!'

'Hurray!'

The driver, looking lardy-faced, turned on his heel, scrambled nimbly into the cab, threw the gears violently, stalled the engine, started it up again, and, amidst a ripple of cheering and beating umbrellas, slowly reversed, churning up as much of the ground as he possibly could, and leaving behind him a choking stench of diesel by way of punishment.

'Round one!' I said to Belle. I felt extraordinarily excited.

'We must fetch a policeman,' said Belle. 'They mustn't be allowed to intimidate people like that!'

I hadn't really thought that a dawn shift would be necessary. Indeed, I'd fervently hoped that it wouldn't. I left Belle at the police-station, did the shopping, and had a late lunch at the back of the shop. People kept coming in all afternoon to talk about the siege of Bunyan's Elm including a reporter from the *Echo*. The fact that I'd been seen with Belle who, with Miss Eddowes, was considered one of the leaders, had apparently put me straight into the rank of the militants.

Oh God! Oh God! Oh God! Every time I surfaced that afternoon I thought of Hughie and how fed up and furious he'd be. It was, of course, entirely my own fault.

'Is Mrs Shafto a close friend of yours?'

'No!'

'Miss Kinoull, may I ask you how you came to identify with her over this?'

'I can't honestly remember.'

'Miss Kinoull, do you intend extending your activities to, say, factory farming?'

'No!'

'I believe that Mrs Shafto is also very concerned about that. Now, Miss Kinoull, do you think that today's citizen is in serious danger of losing his or her control over their environment?'

'I'd have thought they'd lost control of it long ago.'

'You think there's no hope then?'

'No! I mean yes! I don't know!'

'Did you ever belong, like your friend Mrs Shafto, to C.N.D.?'

'No!'

Pollution. Poverty. D.D.T. C.N.A. C.S. Gas. B.B.C. Rubber bullets. Racialism. Illiteracy. Rhodesia. Transplants. Ibos. The 11-plus. Abortion. E.E.C. L.S.D. D.T.S. S.E.B. I.R.A. S.T.S.

'No! No! No! No!'

I got so exhausted that I closed the shop early. Yet I kept finding myself wondering how things were going down at the Platt, and I reflected then how terrifying it was that even such a moderate involvement as mine could generate so much passion for a cause.

As I'd forecast the day turned to sleet. All the same, I wanted to see how things were getting on.

Down at the Platt most of the workmen had gone home and the bulldozer was silent. Two women were pouring tea out of a Thermos into paper cups for the new rota who were guarding the tree, and for the tired-looking constable who'd arrived to keep the peace.

'We're fine, dear!' they said when I asked if they wanted anything. 'We're lovely!'

They'd rigged up a kind of shelter in the inner chamber of the tree, which could be reached by squeezing through a narrowish cleft in the trunk. They'd got groundsheets in there, and blankets and a camping-stove, also a lamp and a radio. They looked comfortably dug-in and extremely cheerful.

'Do you think the preservation order'll come soon?'

'Don't know I'm sure, dear.'

'Do you think the men might come and cut down the tree in the middle of the night?'

'I wouldn't know, dear. All I know is that they can't do it while we're in here, and it would take something to get me out through that little old hole I can tell you. I don't even know how I got in in the first place!' They laughed comfortably.

When I got home the telephone was ringing. It was Belle. As far as she knew the dawn shift was still on, though she promised to let me know if there was any change. She was bringing some mulligatawny soup. I said I'd bring Scotch. I also asked her what Hugh thought about it all. She said she didn't know because she'd only seen him for a moment and there hadn't been time to bring him up-to-date. God bless! she said, much too keenly I thought, and rang off.

'Listen, Hugh,' I said when he came that night. 'I've got myself into the most awful mess!'

'So I see,' he said, and handed me the evening paper. It took up two columns on the front page. There was a picture of the tree with the women standing round it, and there was a picture of the bulldozer. Right in the corner you could just make out Belle and me. We were running, and our skirts were right up round our thighs, and it looked as though we weren't wearing brassières. It must have been taken just at the moment when Belle was shouting 'Shame!' because her mouth was wide open.

'My darling!' said Hugh spreading his hands in mock despair.

'Come and have a drink,' I said. 'Come and have a huge one quickly!' Actually he was laughing, but in rather a disturbing way, I thought. Looking back, I think he must have been genuinely amused as well as rather alarmed.

'Whatever possessed you?' he asked. 'Haven't we always agreed that it's fatal to get involved? Especially for you? You see I do know you, darling. I knew all that reserve and detachment, the alienation, was a kind of blind for what you secretly wanted to do.'

'Which was what?'

'Which was to sit and march and boss and shout . . .'

'Shut up, Hugh!'

'Now, something else. I know that a meeting between you and Belle was more or less inevitable, but I don't want this crappy incident to start anything. I simply couldn't stand a *ménage à trois*!'

'What are you living in now, then?'

'From my point of view it's still a *ménage à deux* because Belle doesn't know, and I don't want Belle to know.'

I didn't either. I liked Belle, but all the same I couldn't help feeling nettled at the way he insisted on Belle's continuing ignorance. It seemed, as he expressed it anyway, more for his own convenience than out of any true concern for her heart.

'I can tell you this is a crucial moment,' he said. 'You must disengage from Belle *now*. Although she isn't all that quick to form new relationships because she's always too dam' occupied organising things, when she does make them they are deep, and intense, and final. I know because I'm married to her,' he said, rather smugly I thought. 'You must disengage now. *Now!*'

I knew then that I was going to ruin the evening.

'Hugh, I'm afraid I can't, as you call it, disengage now!'

'?'

'You must believe me, I simply have to get up at three this morning to help her guard that bloody, bloody tree!'

'For God's sake! You don't have to! Cancel it!'

'I can't cancel it. I promised.'

He got up from his chair then and came and knelt on the floor and wound his arms round me.

'Break your promise! My darling, darling girl, don't be so silly. This sort of thing isn't your scene!'

'Oh, Hughie!'

'Break it, there's a good love!'

'No, I can't. What will she think? You're so unscrupulous!'

'It's you who's unscrupulous. You don't seem to realise that you're risking our whole life together. I'm not joking.

You do love me don't you? Then give it up. Let Belle down. People are always letting Belle down. All do-gooders have hides like rhinoceroses because they're used to being let down. She'll forgive you; she always does; but do please let her down now for all our sakes!'

'There's the tree.'

'The tree! What about the tree?'

'It's more than a tree,' I said repeating what Miss Eddowes had said.

'You know as well as I do, *tout passe, tout casse, tout lasse.* All is lost now, anyway.'

'I find the tree important.'

'Don't be so silly. Don't cheat yourself. The affair of the tree is only an outlet for your frustration, perhaps your emotional frustration,' he added quickly.

'Why does Belle care about the tree, then?'

'Belle is different.'

'You mean she isn't frustrated like I am?'

'You could scarcely be making a more deliberate choice,' he said; 'it's just as though you were ending our whole thing here and now, as though you'd willfully decided to kill it.'

'Hughie! Darling Hughie! Don't sulk, don't say that!'

'Ah, but I do say that!'

We had three more whiskies and then I seduced him like the whore I suppose I was. It was more different than it had ever been. It was exciting because of the way he used me, but on reflection afterwards I bitterly resented it.

The alarm went at half-past two. Hugh had long gone, and I was dreaming about him. We were swimming together in an inland sea; there were white reefs running out through clear water, and the chalky cones of submarine mountains stuck up out of the water and were so hot from the sun that you could barely touch them. We seemed to be happy again, and white and heavily scented water-lilies on long long stalks were growing up from the mauve deeps, and they were tangling us together, perhaps drowning us, but it was pleasant, quite painless, in the dream, and unfrightening.

It was extravagantly cold. I put on my sheepskin and took what Hughie and I had left of the Scotch. When I opened the front door the wind felt keen enough to freeze one's face off, and the deserted night was like a firmament of blue glass, Orion spanning it, his stars bright as the glittering trails of a cosmic snail.

I was to meet Belle down at the Platt, and I half ran through Beaudesert's quiet streets, shivering and scourging myself with obscene curses at my weakness, my suggestibility, my hateful female adaptability that had made me do such a thing against all principles. Presently, from quite far away, like the woodcutter's cabin in the forest, I saw what looked like a fire glowing. When I drew closer the glow resolved into two separate lights, the one coming from a brazier of coals which stood outside a portable workman's hut which had been set down beside the now inert bulldozer, the other issuing like gold steam, from a cleft in the doomed tree.

In the hut three men sat playing poker. From the light cast by the red grassy nuts, their faces looked kind. They said good morning and that they'd have asked me to have a cup of tea but for the fact that they were pretty sure there was a kettle on for me in the other camp.

'But we got very good relations with the ladies over there,' they said cheerfully, 'very good relations indeed.' As far as I could see there was no sign of the policeman.

Inside, the tree was transmogrified. It had become, in the lamplight, the fo'c'sle of a whaling ship, a lighthouse, a cave; there was a pleasant smell of newly made coffee, and in a nimbus of cigarette-smoke six women were sitting round a camping stove, their placid faces swaying like rosy buddhas in its light.

'Well done for making it!' came Belle's voice from the brown shadows. 'That means Ena Carter can go.'

'Well, dear, I'm quite sorry to go, I really am. It reminds me of those nice matey days we used to have in the war. I wouldn't have missed it for anything!' She bulked gigantic at the entrance to the tree, squeezed through, only Heaven knew how, to the accompaniment of jocund remarks from the three men in the hut, and waddled off home. I slipped down into her warm place.

'Don't tell me!' I said to Belle. 'The preservation order hasn't come!' Rather to my surprise, she was smoking. Tension, I supposed. It suited her because it made her seem less like a Girl Guide, more adult.

'It'll come in the morning,' she said, and lit my cigarette for me. The atmosphere in the tree trunk was beginning to get thick. 'But there's been no trouble all night, I gather.'

'None at all,' said a voice that I recognised as Lindy Cooper from the dry cleaners. She said that they were ever such nice fellows over the way, and would any of us mind if she turned on her transistor.

Plain chant mysteriously filled the lower tree-trunk for a moment and then yielded to something more secular. It was turned low.

'It was nice of you to come. When I thought it over afterwards I thought how unfair of me to trap you like that.'

'Oh, why?'

'Well, how were you to know what you were being let in for when you came to a meeting that was to do with something quite different from the one you'd been asked to? It's extraordinary how all this has blown up.'

'Yes, it is.'

'Perhaps it's meant!'

Silence fell. I eased back beside her and thought how extraordinary indeed, and I tried to put out of my mind all the unwanted knowledge I possessed, which would keep cramming into it, about Hugh and his habits. For as we are so truly told, to be the lover of one partner in a marriage uncovers devastatingly, the innocent nakedness of the other. I knew Hugh, who knew Belle, who knew Hugh, who knew me. That face, that gravely beautiful face, in all its naïve innocence, was in part mine through Hugh. I mean possessed by me, carnally mine, as were her hands and eyes and other members that I could not see, and did not want to think about.

Trying not to, I yet played about with this idea for a bit, conscious at the same time of how misleadingly secure the external moment can be. Here we were, comfortable in this great tree, she and I sitting beside each other in apparently wholesome and uncomplicated friendship, both dedicated to a purpose. It was only in my head that I knew of the spoiling maggot of truth.

'Another thing I began worrying about was that you might think this was all rather stupid,' said Belle. She spoke softly so as not to overtop the conversation of the other women in the tree and so cause doubts. 'I mean, however passionately one may hold certain views I know one shouldn't try and force others to adopt them.'

I didn't answer. There was nothing I could actually say, because if you suffer from accidie you don't really have views.

'Hugh says I'm too one-track,' Belle went on apologetically, 'but it really is so difficult if you're the kind of person who can't help seeing the obvious thing to do. I think that life is actually so much more simple than people like to pretend. I mean, for instance, if you put your hand in a fire it'll get burnt. You must have put your hand in a fire?'

'In the way you mean? Yes, I have.'

'But you survived it!'

Had I? At this stage it seemed too early to judge.

'You survived,' said Belle, 'because you learned your lesson.' Then suddenly she asked, 'Do you like animals?'

'Moderately,' I said, feeling rather annoyed. It was too like getting to know each other the first night in the dorm.

'I love them, the most innocent, the most exploited. Do you remember the Irish horses?' I did of course. At the time I had simply turned away from reading accounts of their treatment in the continental slaughterhouses. Since then there'd been so much else: panthers flown out of their jungle in eighteen-inch-high boxes; broiler hens; 80,000 cattle a year going through the passes into Italy, never fed, never watered, dying on arrival. There was no end to the wickedness. One was engulfed by it, made impotent by the magnitude of it. 'I went over on the boat from Cork with an Irish mare,' Belle was saying. 'I'll spare telling you what happened to the others,' she went on considerately. 'It was so frightful. Anyway, I went with her to the borders of Poland. Imagine! I somehow saw to it, which I couldn't for most of the others, that she did at least have water so that she could feed her foal.'

'Oh my God!'

'In the end I bought her for far more than she was worth and brought her home. The foal died, but it was all a good thing in the end, because it finally convinced the protection societies.'

'So something was done?'

'I think something can always be done.'

'I'm ashamed to say I didn't do anything. I felt quite a lot, but I didn't do anything.'

'Well, I suppose in my case there was a sort of relief in action, but you see I think it's terribly important to stop that sort of inhumanity, because if people think nothing of treating living creatures like that the day will come, as of course it did in Germany, when people think nothing of doing the same to their fellow men.'

'Have some Scotch,' I said. I found what she was saying depressing.

'I think I'd rather have soup.'

I poured myself a large one and drank it quickly; it was pleasantly fiery.

'I do realise of course that it's just a drop in the ocean. We are hardly moving at all in the enlargement of our humanity. Perhaps only marking time,' she said lighting another cigarette. The smoke that she breathed from her lungs smelt pleasant. God knows what lungs look like, but I imagined hers being clean, filled with something like ozone. The smoke smelt as though it had been somewhere clean.

'You are fortunate to be so active. In the West, anyway, I suppose we're trained to think this desirable, though I'm afraid I am in retreat.'

'In retreat?' She didn't really understand.

'I live mostly in the past. Not even in the real past either—a past without its stink, and I don't make the slightest attempt to realise it.'

'That's a pity if you feel about it so much.'

'It should be "in Earth as it is in Heaven",' I said, 'shouldn't it?'

'That's what I try to tell Hugh.'

'Fortunately I'm not a Christian,' I said.

'Oh, it's so difficult!'

Timeless platitude! There was silence again. It was very hot inside the tree; someone was snoring, and outside an owl screamed, a ratchety hunting scream.

In the most conventional sense Belle was of course too good for Hugh, outrageously too good. Why ever had he married her? And then I reflected that to the corrupt nothing is more sexually attractive than the virtuous—to begin with, that is to say, and until boredom sets in . . . I closed my eyes. Belle's head had dropped rather painfully on to my shoulder . . .

Then, quite suddenly there was the sound of a lorry approaching, and shortly afterwards an outbreak of men's voices. The engine was left running, and the lorry was so close that you could smell the exhaust coming through the hole in the tree-trunk. In a matter of moments all six of us had scrambled through this cleft, and, like farrowed piglets, we emerged yawning and coughing from the grateful warmth of the tree's womb into the flaying cold of the early morning air.

There were eight men including the three watchmen in the hut. One of them, with his foot braced against it, was already yanking at the starting string of a chain saw.

'What are you going to do?' we shouted at a man who looked as though he might be the gaffer.

'The lower branches have got to be trimmed up if it's going to stay,' he said.

'What! At this time in the morning! Come on, girls! Where's the policeman?' But the words were drowned as the chain saw screamed into life.

'Come on, girls! Backs to the tree!'

So once again the old tree was encircled by the dry-cleaning woman, the chemist's wife, two women I'd never seen before, Belle Shafto and me. Dawn was showing, actually, as I think Hardy was derided for describing it, like a dead baby, blue-white, flaccid-looking, chill, as we stood, my heart pumping with fright and excitement, our ungloved hands thawing into each other's.

For a few moments, but for only a few, the workmen tried to jostle us aside in order to get the ladder up against the trunk so that they could reach the lower branches. But they honestly hadn't a chance. By mistake one of them stood with his great boot on the chemist's wife's foot, and she let out such a piercing yell that he suddenly went pale round his nose as though he were going to be sick, and backed off. Then an early-morning bus taking the cleaning ladies to the chemical weapons factory stopped, and all the cleaning ladies got out and gathered round and began jeering at the workmen, which unnerved them still more, so that quite shortly they stopped trying to get the ladder up the tree at all and tried arguing instead. They were nice men, anyway, and their hearts hadn't really been in the thing from the start.

The preservation order arrived half an hour later. Miss Eddowes brought it. She waved it in the air and everyone went mad and began cheering—us, and the busload of cleaning ladies, even the chain-saw men who were sick of the whole business by now. Then we all danced round the tree, because it seemed the obvious thing to do. We sang 'Under the Spreading Chestnut Tree', though it was actually an elm that we'd saved; then we sang 'Knees up, Mother Brown' for no particularly good reason, and then we sang that hideously embarrassing song called 'The Hokey Cokey'. Everyone looked very tribal doing it, I thought, swaying and prostrating themselves and genu-flecting in front of the Bunyan Elm as though it were some kind of god. I had to do it too, and in the end I enjoyed myself. Then we gave three cheers for the preservation order, after which we all kissed one another, we who had been round the tree: the two strange women, the chemist's wife, and lastly dear, noble Belle. She hurt me she squeezed so much, and as she did so I remembered what Hugh had said about not getting involved.

FOUR

'It could work,' I said, 'there's no earthly reason why it shouldn't.'

'Except that it never works,' said Hugh.

It was April, and we were discussing our *ménage à trois*. I had already got used to it. Time in its rather shocking way seems to normalise practically everything. As an aunt of mine used to say, you can get used to anything in this world but the bastinado. Unfortunately this didn't seem to apply to Hugh. His lack of adaptability was now beginning to look very like obstinacy and I said so.

'It would be so much easier if you didn't see Belle,' he kept saying sulkily. 'It's almost impossible to make you understand, but when you see Belle it makes me feel naked, as though there wasn't a corner of this earth left for me to creep into.'

'But I hardly ever see Belle.'

'You've seen her three times at least.'

'You're not jealous?'

'Don't be ridiculous.'

'I don't feel that I can stop seeing Belle entirely,' I said, 'after that tree incident, I mean. We went through quite a lot together then, you know.'

'No comment,' Hugh said.

I didn't want to stop seeing Belle. I was drawn to Belle, not violently drawn, for I'm not a violent sort of person, but definitely drawn all the same. On those few occasions that we'd met since the Bunyan Elm business it had been borne in on me that, although Belle's belief that one can literally always do something to improve things in this life might in fact turn out to be an illusion, it was by and large more cheering illusion than Hugh's truth. At least with Belle there was an impression of movement. Things did at least appear to be happening, and this, after Hugh's elegant but adamantine pessimism, was unexpectedly grateful to me. I needed Hugh's view too, of course. Laughter of the kind he provoked was far too precious a gift to lose.

Belle and I had probably met three or four times since the tree, sometimes by chance, once or twice to discuss matters arising from the Bunyan Elm victory. I had been persuaded, and not all that unwillingly, by both Belle and Miss Eddowes, to take on some of the publicity for their Preservation Society. I had agreed to find a speaker on aspects of local history. There was to be a photograph exhibition of local horrors on the one hand, local beauty spots on the other, and I'd found that all the tragic information I'd been hugging to myself, brooding over, wounding myself with again and again (the old almshouses that had been made into a garage, the filled-in village duck-pond, etc.) could be used by Belle and Miss

Eddowes—creatively. I didn't tell Hugh about this. Not only would it have provided a further stick with which he would take a delight in beating me, but I had to allow myself time to take in my own defection from previous principles. I also forebore to tell Hugh something else, and this was that a kind of childish mock relationship had already begun to develop between Belle and me. It sprang, of course, from our very different views about life, so that, like the swaying Lorenz geese who have so sensibly evolved a ritual elegant as that at the court of the Sun King, we evolved something much less elegant, to resolve our differences—something that Hugh, had he got wind of it, would have mocked unmercifully and deservedly, for there is never much wit between women when they get on their own. It was a kind of formula to avoid embarrassment. I blush to repeat it. In acknowledgement of what she pretended were my highly reactionary views Belle called me Comrade. I, for obvious reasons, retorted by calling her La Marchesa.

'When are you going to see Belle again?'

'I don't know.'

'Thank God!' He became quite cheerful. I wanted to tell him how very much I loathed this kind of cross-questioning that he'd gone in for recently, for it heaped upon me the most complicated feelings of double, of treble guilt.

'I can't help it if she rings me up,' I said. 'She's usually the one who gets into touch with me, you know; it's nearly always that way round.'

'Yes, I know, sweet one,' he said trying hard, 'I know you can't always help it.'

'Of course you were right,' I said, moved by his attempt at generosity to be generous myself, 'I should never have become involved in the beginning.'

Now that I knew Belle better I had become even more anxious that she shouldn't find out about Hugh and me. I would have been so sad for that dear, kind, Nordic innocent to suffer. I would have hated it. Strangely enough the fact that I was deceiving her didn't seem to spoil our meetings at all. I seemed, in a way that was both odd and frightening, simply to be able to ignore my own treachery when I was with her, as though her very presence truly made the very idea of such a thing impossible, cancelled it out. I often found myself wondering whether Hugh had had these very feelings when he was betraying her with me. So normal-seeming was Belle's and my friendship that there were times when I almost felt I could tell her about Hugh and me, and that it wouldn't make any kind of difference, so then we could all really be a *ménage à trois*, but in the open, and life would become as uncomplicated and Edenic as it ought to be. After all, I was used to sharing Hugh with her, I had done so from the beginning. Surely we were all civilised enough now to overstep the foolish tribal taboos which dogged us in the name of 'marriage'? And yet I hesitated. Belle very much loved Hugh. Such thoughts were dangerous. We were not in Heaven yet, and, alas, there were still marriages.

'My Rococo Symposium is fixed for May 15th,' Hugh said. 'Rosa's beside herself at the idea of an invasion by *hoi polloi*.'

'Poor Rosa! She cares too much.'

'It's really worst,' Hugh suddenly said taking my hand and gently slipping his fingers between mine, 'about Belle,

I mean, when she asks you home. You must forgive me, darling, but I do find it so utterly disorientating.'

'It's certainly not how lovers and mistresses should behave,' I agreed. 'Mistresses should live tucked away in secret love-nests, I know. But actually I've only been to you twice, and the first time you weren't even there!'

He hadn't been. Belle Shafto had been insistent over the phone, difficult in terms of excuse to resist. In any case, as it happened, I hadn't wanted to resist. This time for a wonder it was nothing to do with pollution or exploitation or birth control.

'I'd like you to see my mother-in-law's place,' she said. 'It's the best example I know of a blunder being turned into a beauty, if you know what I mean. She won't be there herself, but she said, Bring anyone you like, so I'm taking Jessica and the Young Citizens, and if you'd like to . . .'

'I honestly don't know about the Young Citizens,' I said. 'What sort of body are they?'

'You mustn't be prejudiced. Comrade Herovshka!'

'La Marchesa commanda!'

Belle rowed us over to the largest island in Mrs Shafto's dinghy. It had been newly varnished, its treacly sides sticky as toffee, and it just held us, five immaculate Young Citizens, Belle's daughter and me.

'They were the group who collected more waste-paper than anyone else,' explained Belle. 'Off the streets you know; Beaudesert's getting so filthy.'

'Young Stakhanovites!' I said. The Young Citizens were staring glassily ahead. I'd seen them picking up paper, though not off the Beaudesert streets but out of my dust-bins, and stuffing it into their plastic sacks.

As we landed, a warm wind was blowing, and from the small boat grinding into the shallows you could see through the trees to where primroses and white wood anemones were coming out under the cherry trees.

'Small twigs first,' Belle instructed the Young Citizens sternly, 'then bigger.' She was exceedingly thorough, because in the end the Young Citizens got sick of it and we had to light the fire ourselves with paper.

'It's very important to train them properly with fires,' said Belle staring down into the frying pan where in fat, clear as spring water, the obdurately un-browning sausages lay sullenly like amputated cows' tits. The children had mooned off to pick things, their voices diminishing. Belle pulled the stopper out of a bottle of Chassepré.

'How noble to take on the Young Citizens,' I said.

'I rather like it,' said Belle. 'Strength through Joy, Comrade!' she added.

'That's the wrong party,' I said, 'though it doesn't matter!' She smiled, unoffended, and I lay back in the grass and listened to the sausages whining in their pan, and behind that to the sound of waves lapping against the side of the boat, and reflected how starved I'd actually been of female companionship. Ever since I'd left school, trained, and been in business, I'd lived most of the time with men. Living with a man as opposed to a husband tends to preclude female friendships, or so I've found, so there's a sense in which it would seem odd for me to share any sort of a home with a woman now. For in these past years, when I haven't been living with a man, I've preferred to live alone, with the result that women, except in the most superficial sense, have become strangers to me. I've forgotten what they

like doing, what they like eating and talking about, matters in which men are completely familiar to me. There are
other things I've forgotten too, the peculiar, rather unfunny
things women laugh at, and the way they can be so easy-
going and uncritical, not minding if you change direction
suddenly, because they do themselves: and how kind and
considerate they are as a matter of course, because it's always
expected of them, and how, except sometimes in practical
matters, they are not always striving to be dominant or to
tell you things, being so used, I can only suppose, to being
dominated. I thought of all this as I lay listening to the
waves and the sausages, and I thought how agreeable it was
to be picnicking here with Belle and the Young Citizens,
untrammelled, for once, by lovers or business.

'What's your mother-in-law like?' I asked. I suppose
it was a measure of the degree to which we had already
become familiar that I could even ask Belle this. In family
matters Belle was both loyal and reserved, almost to a fault.

'Hugh finds her difficult,' Belle said. 'It's hard to say
exactly why. He says she's overshadowed him all his life,
and I can see what he means. She's one of those people with
an appalling amount of energy.'

'That's hardly her fault.'

'No, of course not. She's simply an upper-class casualty.'

It was on the tip of my tongue to say that nothing
Hugh had said about his mother remotely suggested casualty, and then I refrained, but only just in time.

'Too young to have hit emancipation,' said Belle, 'married too young to enjoy its benefits.'

'Has she turned into "a mother of men"? I know
quite a number of frustrated women who visit their

disappointment with the world upon their sons, who in their turn vent it upon other women.'

'Not exactly. That's to say, I can't make up my mind whether it's being the mother of sons or just really rather mannish. She has a powerful personality.'

'How odd that one always defines strong women in terms of men.'

'Is it? I suppose it is.'

'Do you get on with her?'

'I admire her,' said Belle guardedly. 'But I don't like her crushing Hugh. She exhausts Hugh. Poor Hugh!'

'How exactly does she exhaust Hugh?'

'By her sheer presence, it seems. You probably don't realise it, but Hugh's rather lazy, and his mother's always doing things. You know, enormous projects like all this,' Belle waved her hand round the trees. 'It makes Hugh feel so guilt-ridden and indolent. I mean she loves heaving stones and earth about, felling trees, altering things, making things . . .'

'You make her sound like a sort of cramped minor goddess. One of the once powerful Eumenides, demoted now and looking for something to do!'

'Nonsense!' cried Belle. 'There's plenty she could do if she wanted to. The whole world's waiting for her to do something.'

'Geriatrics. Spastics. Tantrics!'

'Shut up!'

'Hysterics!'

The children were returning.

When they had thoroughly ravaged the picnic basket we all rose and played 'Guard the Tree'.

Mothers are used to these games, of course. I wasn't. I'd been oscillating for so long between lovers and business that I'd forgotten an entire dimension of childhood living, and, like most childish people, I desired to please in the matter of games, to excel, even if in trying too hard I made a fool of myself. In that paling spring evening I rolled down my stockings so that they shouldn't get laddered by brambles and then I cast care utterly to the winds. I went pounding and thundering through Mrs Shafto's little copses, breaking off her young branches, tearing my flesh as I pursued the shrieking little mice boys and girls. Once I cornered one, and there was a death chase as he doubled back and ran over a peninsula of soft grass until, balked by a tree fallen in the spring gales, we took madly to the water. Cruelly intent on my mouse boy, I churned through the dark water, soaking myself to the waist in my frenzy, and in the end, choking with laughter, I caught him, glossy and wet and fluttering as a young starling.

Belle I hardly saw in the course of this particular game, and when I did she always seemed to be crashing rather aimlessly through the undergrowth like a great amiable elephant, driving shrieking children before her. She didn't seem to be trying very hard, which I thought was bad for the children. By the time it was our turn to hide it was late; the air had turned chill, and in the darkening evening a small rindy moon was shining through a slit in the sky, not giving much light, which was just as well because Belle, as I might have guessed from her previous performance, turned out to be too big and honest to be much good at self-concealment. The chase with the mouse boy had actually made me forget my size for the time being, and once again I was myself a child, deadly savage, inching my way on elbows and knees through the indigo jungle to warn Belle. She was standing out, big and white, a natural victim for the vicious shrimps who even now were cutting their counting and fanning out along the cold watery rim of the island for the kill. I edged towards her in the poor light, wanting to warn her to get down. I hissed softly, but she continued to stand, unaware, absently smiling. The light, vicious crackling of the hunting children grew closer. Unseen in the dusk, they moved in. I reached Belle at last and touched her leg. She flinched and drew in her breath (what on earth could she have been thinking about?), but didn't scream. I pulled at her skirt and made her kneel down in the wet grass. She made a wry face but didn't say anything. There was more crackling, much nearer now, and then a Young Citizen came quietly out of the trees and stood three feet away from us, nostrils flaring, turning with slow careful movements of the head to left and right, sniffing slightly as though trying to catch the scent of us. He surely couldn't fail to hear the animal beating of my heart. He moved away a few feet, walking daintily down a narrow ride between the hazels, then stopped again. We watched him, motionless, and then there was an extraordinary sound, rather like a muffled fart. I felt the muscles of Belle's wrist tighten suddenly. In a second or two she began to shake. For a moment I thought she must be having some kind of fit, and then I realised that she was laughing, or really trying to stifle laughter. And then that mad, delightful panic, that true hysteria which afflicts schoolgirls, and sometimes grown women too, seized me, and together, for a moment, we shook and rocked, trying in agony to bottle up the great earth-shaking whoop. But it came, irrepressibly like tumultuous water, bursting, rushing from our throats, the brassy, braying din of it exploding the demure spring night.

They were on us in an instant, screaming, laughing, pinching, scratching, with the terrifying vigour of hunting animals: and in a moment we all became one writhing, giggling, tender animal lashing its strength about in the dark on the wet grass, shamefully crushing shoots, cracking boughs, until I became aware, but not before Belle did, of someone calling across the water.

'Oh God,' said Belle, 'it's Hugh's mother! Shut up! Shut up! Ssh!'

We got up, and even in the poor light I could see that there were leaves and branches littered all over the place and scattered flower petals. The children, suddenly subdued, picked up their packages and scuttled towards the boat.

'Will she be furious?' I asked as I pushed off. Wisely, probably, Belle didn't answer. Disapproval emanating from somewhere on the other side of the island seemed to pervade the night. It became darker. We rounded the island, and as Belle dipped the oars I could just see, on the far bank, a dumpy figure waiting for us. Small as it was, it seemed monolithic as we jerked over the water to meet it.

'Don't beach it!' called out a gruff voice. 'Bring her over to the jetty and I'll tie her up.'

When we reached the jetty, Hugh's mother didn't say anything. She just bent down and tied the painter in a swift competent-looking knot. I couldn't see her face properly because it was almost dark, but in reflected light from the water I could see her hands. They were lean and nimble-looking for an elderly woman, and when she helped us out with our cargo of carrier-bags and rubbish, I could feel they were strong as well.

'If I weren't so put out about the trees you've broken, I'd ask you in for a drink,' she said to Belle in the darkness. 'You and your friend.'

'I'm sorry about the trees,' said Belle. 'This is Hero Kinoull.'

I felt Mrs Shafto assessing me, which was difficult owing to the darkness. I knew instinctively that she summed me up as an invader, though I felt that she would have liked me inside so that she could have a good look at my eyes.

'It's nice of you. Gran, but we mustn't stay for a drink,' continued Belle evenly. The attention was off me now, and it was a simple case of these two women, who already knew each other, feeling their way back to their conventional harmony.

'I'm afraid we stayed too late,' Belle said, 'and then the children got rather over-excited, but they all had such a lovely time.'

'It sounded as though they had a lovely time,' said Mrs Shafto dryly. 'Well, come and have a drink another time. Any time, I'm always here, you know that, you and Miss Kinoull.'

So at the end of that spring night it looked as though I'd gathered to me not only Hugh and Hugh's wife and child, but Hugh's mother as well, and it seemed to me, in the rather overblown frame of mind I was in then, that at a stroke I could deprive the child of a father, the wife of a husband, the mother of a son.

'It'll get worse,' Hugh prophesied. 'There'll be minute adjustments here and there, and in the end you'll come to and you won't recognise who or what you are.' And then, exacting payment for my treachery I suppose, he made love to me, if you could call it that, as roughly and selfishly as he knew how and as though I were already another person. Yet, looking back, I suppose I must see that this was a kind of acceptable, if ungainly, release for us both, he screwing away his fear and anger and I being purged, I suppose, of my guilt.

'What do you want me to do then?' I'd asked him. 'Do you want me to go?'

'You can't go,' he said. 'You know I'd die of misery if you went. You can't go now.'

I knew of course that he didn't want me to go, and in any case I didn't want to go myself. Like him, I wanted to drift on in helpless but sweet anguish, just waiting to see what would happen.

I also continued to see Belle Shafto. If you'd asked me why, I'd have found it hard to say. A kind of fascinated guilt played some part in it, I think. There was also that illusion, which I always had when I was with her, of normality and innocence, and the combination of this, together with my knowledge of how matters really stood, was, for some reason, irresistible. It was like living in two dimensions at once; it was like perpetually experiencing that moment of first biting into the fruit of the tree of knowledge.

I must also add that I tried, as I'd promised Hugh, to let Belle make the occasion and not me, though I admit I was not always so scrupulous about this as I made out to

Hugh. Occasions for meeting Belle simply grew naturally and spontaneously from the meeting before, and I didn't seek to discourage them.

But I had to pacify Hugh after these outings, and if I was planning some future venture with Belle I had to bribe him. An afternoon with Belle cost a whole evening, sometimes a night, with Hugh. I hated this because payment in sex diminishes capacity, and although women can, with very little trouble, conceal and simulate so much, it was psychologically exhausting. But I had begun to be afraid that if I didn't comply, not only would I not see Belle but that Hugh, in a tantrum, would blow the gaffe and tell Belle we were lovers, and I didn't want that. So I spent far too much time away from the shop and away from sales, achieving nothing, nothing, only an extremely strong and pleasurable sexo-spiritual anguish which was quite new to me.

Time, however, as it does with everything, normalised even this, as it had already normalised my situation *vis-à-vis* Belle, as it was even then normalising those highly abnormal evenings we three began to spend together, for how could I now refuse endlessly to dine with them both at their flat in Beaudesert?

It may have been the mercurial weather of that restlessly advancing spring that played upon my hapless indolence, but to me these seemed such doomed, glamorous evenings, the fatal aura of the past already upon them. They were evenings pregnant with their own utterly needless tragedy, yet tragedy for all that, so that with each passing moment the full poignancy of personality must be doubly, triply relished. Perversely enough I found that

I felt far closer to Hugh, far more in love with him, in Belle's presence. It seemed that he and I between us were safeguarding Belle's happy innocence, enabling her, by our own rough, anguished love, to play, unimpeded, like a child in a butterfly world. Surprisingly we often laughed openly, Hugh and I, at Belle, at her enthusiasms, at her politics, at her artlessness. This made her exceedingly happy. There are people who seem to flourish when others are the sympathetic witnesses of their shortcomings. They gain immensely in confidence, especially if the shortcomings are seen humorously and tenderly, and, as I have said, Hugh and I saw Belle's shortcomings humorously and tenderly, and in our tender humour she flourished. We three became unspeakably close, and there seemed no bounds to Belle's happy innocence, or unawareness, or what some people might have called her stupidity, and I straddled over their marriage it seemed, like a victorious colossus. Yet I was also a victim.

Sometimes, when I lay alone at night, I would tell myself, and I would know its truth, that I had fallen into that fatal, fatal trap which Buddha adjures the wise to avoid at all costs. I speak of that testing plain that we must traverse after our death, a plain littered, we are told, with copulating creatures, with flowers and butterflies and human beings, which the soul, sick for love of Earth, longs to embrace. It is a temptation the soul must fight against, for if it succumbs it will be caught firmly between the male and female principles, and willy-nilly be born again, to live out another tedious incarnation. In my victim moods, lying alone, it seemed that through my own good nature I had done exactly this, had embraced and been trapped, vice-like, between a rutting couple, and must now suffer a hideous re-birth.

And this in a manner of speaking is precisely what happened only a month after the picnic that ended so unfortunately on Mrs Shafto's island.

FIVE

Here I am on my way to a furniture sale. I should be at the shop, of course; the assistant and the cat are fed up with my repeated absences, but the weather is too beautiful for work: besides, Belle wants a kitchen table for the children's nursery. Belle is driving.

We've just gone through Aylesbury; the hood is down and I'm so deafened by the wind rushing past that I have to ask her to repeat whatever it is she's just said:

'I didn't say anything!'

Huge black sunglasses mask the upper portion of her face. Below her straight Britomart nose, the lower half lives its own calm life. Firm, well-moulded, unrouged lips curl and smile over the good unstopped white teeth; there are the faint beginnings of lines at the corners of her mouth—caused through smiling so much? or pursing her lips in good-natured acquiescence? I don't know. The impression is of a mouth both tender and patient. The hands at quarter to three on the wheel are large and white and look competent with their clean, short-buffed nails. Their only vanity is an enormous crested agate taken from a man's fob and transformed into a ring for her marriage finger. Hugh's crest? I look back (and this happens all in the space of the moment in which I am waiting to hear her say 'I didn't say anything!') to her patient mouth. There is down on her upper lip, very fair, and through its nimbus I can see two black and white cows in a field, licking each other . . . and then quite without warning a frightful sensation, pain or sickness, but actually neither, runs up from the ticklish pit of my belly to my throat and then, in a kind of flaming cross, penetrates viciously outwards to my nipples, throbbing there for a second or two.

Angina! It's gone as suddenly as it has come, like all dangerous pains. Wind. Belle, oblivious, drives on. Gallstones! But I must have been mistaken. I could only have imagined a pain like that.

We slow down suddenly at traffic lights. We've been going too fast. Neatly Belle double-declutches. I happen to be looking at the floor, wondering whether I did actually have the astounding pain I thought I had, or whether I hadn't. The neat strong ankle, clean as the fetlock of a well-bred horse, articulates perfectly; tendons running up the tanned hairless leg cause the cooperating muscles to flex and slacken obediently as the clutch pedal is depressed . . . Then, unmistakably, it is here again. The pain. Only this time in reverse. Cadmium yellow flame tears inwards from my breasts, coalesces in a molten column at my duodenum and then cascades in a golden shower to my lap, turns into what feels like a snared bird, and stays there, pulsing in an extraordinary fashion.

Shock and fear make it difficult for me to sit upright.

'I'm ill!' I think. 'Thank God that my mind's still operating and can tell me that I'm ill. Very, very ill!'

'We're here!' cries Belle braking sharply and turning with a spurt of gravel through entrance gates of plum-coloured brick topped by grey stone gryphons. We sweep grittily over a weedy overhung drive which debouches with malicious suddenness before an architecturally chaotic house. Belle gets out.

'Do you mind if I wait in the car for five minutes?' I say.

'What's the matter? Of course not!' Belle leans solicitously over the side of the car, and, removing her great sunglasses, peers anxiously at me, so that I can see my own shrunken reflection in the blue well of her eyes. 'Are you all right?'

'Yes! Yes! Yes! Yes!' I cry, longing for her to go. 'It's only that you drove rather fast. I'm feeling a bit squeamish. I'll follow you in!'

She has barely disappeared inside the hideous front door before I am overtaken by a new sensation. Warm air, pungent as ether, seems to be entering deliciously my lower bowels, expending shamelessly the nervous, shrunken maps of private regions which are located there, expanding them into a soft, insistently swelling landscape. In me are high, feathered poplars moving gently against sun-swelled clouds, and willows rapturously trailing gold leaves in a dark steam: and close by there's a strange plant in whose slowly opening petals I can see moon-coloured stamens arching their trembling peppery anthers. It is a landscape whose sharp springs, welling over into pools, warm and green as at Clitumnus, spill again into water-meadows, which engulf to the belly the fat white oxen browsing there in the high grass, and then they run away in bright welling streams to the deep river which, inexorably flowing, causes my legs, inert marble as they have become, to sag apart in order to admit of its enormous dark sweetness.

'This isn't normal!' I say aloud but quietly as I sit there on the burning seat-leather of Belle's car. Around me, seeming to echo that growing sweetness between my legs, the air is expanding with the loud singing of birds.

I light a cigarette, comforting myself that so much nowadays is really only glandular. Then my mind runs off at a tangent, and I recollect reading somewhere that this sort of thing usually happens to hairdressers because they are all herded together in a hot spicy unhealthy atmosphere and see far too much of each other and that's why. Yet this hardly applies to me who have a lover, and whose assistant at the shop as well as whose cat are both men, and no end of people coming into the shop anyway. Then I remember that Hugh and I haven't been sleeping together so much and perhaps that's why.

Yet, at the back of my mind, I am not deluded. The truth of it is like the awful revelation of having the curse for the first time, or perhaps it's more what it would be like if someone told you you had only got three months to live. Unacceptable. Unbelievable. Yet with its own irrefutable symptoms.

I smoke my cigarette right down to its butt. Then I test to see how things are getting on. My legs still feel like inert marble, but the sweet continents that have unfolded between them, all the flowers and bells and birds and waxy, Eastern-smelling magnolia petals, have contracted, thankfully, to one small warm ogden melon. I open the car door. Gaining confidence I covertly practise walking backwards and forwards once or twice. All is well, and I go off to find Belle.

The idea of a sale in a house moves me. It always has done, even though I'm used to sales, this death of a way of life. Even now, passing through the rooms, looking for the kitchen, where Belle's table will surely be, I take in by force of habit those marks that annotate the past life: the dog scratches which spoil the doors, old spills on carpets, finger marks round light-switches. Scribbles, so intimate, so indicative, soon to be scribbled over in their turn. So I traipse, a kind of gas-powered revenant, to the kitchen.

Belle has already bought her table, which surprises me. It means that I must have been sitting outside in the car for much longer than I'd thought. She is even now giving the man instructions about having the table sent by carrier to Beaudesert. When she sees me she becomes all solicitude again. Women are so charming in this way; they don't just ask you once how you are and have done, like a man; they keep on asking you, matily charting your progress with you. Just at the moment, however, I don't want this kindness because I am so very afraid that what I have at last recognised has happened to me will go and happen again if Belle goes on being so kind.

It was okay, however, perfectly okay. We had a cup of tea and then went back to the car to go home, and although I now felt normal as anything and the worrying and beautiful Xanadu garden had vanished without trace from my secret regions, the map rolled up, I was careful all the way home to look out of the window just in case it could happen again.

And it did, quite unambiguously, just as we were driving through the Woburn Safari Park. I was not even looking at Belle. And so at last I knew for certain.

Now it was that my days, once so evenly and pleasantly divided between the twin interests of Hugh and the shop, became instead frenziedly, paradisially unbalanced by phantasies.

Appearance and actuality part company altogether. I inhabit strange countries now. Here I am in my workroom at the back of the shop; my workroom which I love, with its press and its paper-cutter and its rolls of binding-gauze and buckram, and its own smell, which sends me, of book glue and the hot peppery smell of heated tooling dies. My room, which looks out on to my own dear sunlit garden with the mulberry tree cradled in its padded iron support spreading its green shade, patterning with the moving shadows of its rough leaves my stone urn with the satyrs' heads, and raining, in midsummer, its delicious raspberry-like fruit on to the grass. And here am I heating up the tools, stamping in gold-leaf willows and singing birds and suns and moons and stars along the spines of the books. I can see my hands moving with nimble love, but they seem like someone else's hands, not mine any more. Indeed it is true, for I am watching a husk, a cocoon from which the imago, the central 'I', has left long ago, leaving a mere earthly 'she' patiently embossing gold suns on the book-spines, while outside, beneath the opening buds of the mulberry tree, the blackbirds trill and mute.

I am meanwhile girdling the earth, defeating time, like Ariel.

I am a parhelion, I am a shell-thin alabaster sphere filled with fire and myrrh. I poise and I drop, breaking open my precious phial, and the contents mix with the earth, become incarnate, the myrrh and the fire which, now man, now woman, I carry always in my breast. So that sometimes I am an Egyptian prince, my brick-red body burning beneath its layer of zephyrous gauze, my boat moving amongst the rattling green pipes of the Nile reeds. The boat rocks as the tailless swimming cats plunge grinning over the side to retrieve the fallen duck, and I press my lips to the soft splashed inner-arm of the princess, who is water to my fire, moon to my sun, echo for my wild singing. And sometimes I lie, in another age, another place, where the water susurrates through the gravel of little stones, Ssh! and Ssh! a woman again, rocked in the radiant arms of a man with eyes as blue as the Marchesa's, sheltered by his hair from the sunlight which drops like running honey through the broad thin-veined leaves. Or else the sun goes in, and the aurora rages like a coloured wind in the dark sky, and with the scent of oozing pine resin in my nostrils I lie by the savage crackling of a fire, wrapped in a white bearskin, no longer a man nor a woman, but one whole with my other. White, secret, warm, locked.

These were the regions I inhabited; this is what I did and what I was, while she who was Hero Kinoull bound her books and sold them efficiently enough to support that glorious imago; also carefully digested and eliminated what she ate, and talked to people until such time as phantasy and actuality, like brutally parted constituents, ran passionately together and became one again, which was when I was with Belle.

I submitted utterly to my passionate illness. Insomuch as the majesty of a god is said to arise from a spoonful of non-intoxicant wine, a segment of dry wafer, so but to see Belle, if only for a few moments, to speak to her on the telephone even, became the incarnation of those phantasies which had kept me stravaging like a lunatic through the vastness of the creation.

Belle remained totally unaware. So unaware that any-one but an infatuate might have been excused for thinking her unfeeling. I can't say that I didn't experience a slight lowering of temperature about this from time to time, but then, as with most things in life, the reverse coin of Belle's dreadful unawareness brought its own compensation. I was free, far freer than most people in a similar predica-ment, to indulge myself absorbedly, upon things like the perfect shell-like convolutions of the ears; the peerless lift of the eyebrows that were like the glossy wings of a wheat-coloured bird; the entrancing way the firm lips curved when she spoke, all those things in fact which lovers con-tinue to talk about. I was also safer than most to cherish her abandoned, happy scarves (she was very untidy) which came my way when she left them in my car or in the flat. They smelt mildly of clean hair, and her jackets, whose pockets I searched for any tiny but important revelation of character, yielded only Biros, address-books, crumpled bills and tickets, but with these I was content. Oh, per-fectly content, so odd, removed, feeding-on-air is this sort of love. And even in my phantasies I never came to any central point. I mean I never imagined a consummation of any kind. I was there already. 'Before Abraham was I am' was the sum of it. It was not that I did not dare; it was unnecessary. So my phantasies were those of being 'there', like that kind moment when the act of love is over and you are resting, fitting into each other, as Colette once said, like spoons in a box, waiting to sleep. So I dreamed of landscapes in which I lived with her, of gardens in the past or the present or the future where, as in a vision from Isaiah, there was no cold nor strife, nor dying nor being born any more, but only a long, June afternoon.

Yet, as on that first day at the furniture sale when this thing struck me out of the blue, I had surprisingly lucid moments when, unlike some possessed people, I was somehow able to inquire objectively what on earth had actually happened to me. To this end I scribbled a kind of journal in an old account book.

Outside May tumbles and shouts in great gouts of white flowers, in breakers of leaves. 'Is this an endocrine disturbance?' I ask myself carefully. 'Memo the hens you once read about, one so stimulated by absence of cock that it grew wattles and spurs and began crowing and treading others! . . . Is this some deep psychological regression then? I mean caused by mother and father both being killed in Borneo when I was only a few years old and that old fool Aunty Do bringing me up so slackly? What about an analyst? Would take three years at least and be terribly expensive. Do I want an analyst? Belle. Character of Belle. A sort of sweet fool, a grown-up schoolgirl, a girl guide, childish as well as childlike, really knows nothing of the world in spite of being married to Hugh and having children. I suppose if I weren't infatuated I'd have to call her rather stupid, but then to the corrupt, saints and angels are stupid. *Her effect on me apart from the obvious*'—I underline this heavily in red. 'Life, ordinary Life is just folding up. In a way, her own way, she's corrupting *me*. Not her fault, of course. Corrupting me, not physically, that's just some joke of the gods; she's corrupting me mentally. Perhaps in the end you just can't separate mentally from physically. My whole way of thinking seems to be changing. From being a retired Romantic with a passion for the past and not much hope in the future, she's turning me into an active *participant,* someone *involved,* a sort of progressive with a modern conscience. *Her* moral conscience. Christ must work through society, she tells me. Not because I am intellectually convinced, but because I love her so much, the up-until-now meaningless wailings about pollution, compensatory eating, threatened oryx, tower flats, are separating out, and becoming attached to blood and flesh and personality, are becoming, in her terrible jargon, I have to say it, meaningful. I hate this. I hate this virtue which is dependent upon the desires of my heart. Yet I keep remembering that it's not her fault. She would say, I think, that it was God moving in his mysterious way, making himself manifest even if through perversity and passion.'

'I bet you haven't remembered?' On the telephone.

'Marchesa dear, what haven't I remembered?'

'Now try and think!' I could hear her laughing at the end of the wire. With one part of me I could hear that her laughter was rather brassy, without much humour; with another part, the enslaved part, it belled in my ears like the laughter of the Nile Princess.

'Hyde Park, silly! Remember?'

'Oh no!'

'You'll pick me up nine-ish then? It's just us!'

'Just us?' I repeated stupidly wondering whether poor Hugh was listening.

'God bless!' she said. 'Goodbye now!'

The day shone gold as well-drawn cider. As golden for tainted as for whole love, which always seems so extraordinary, though perhaps it really is only the mind which insists on wrenching apart truth and appearance.

'I must just go through my notes,' said the Marchesa. She read them absorbed, unseeing, magnificently and barbarously uncaring. We were tearing through a landscape which was the reflection of my love for her; those beautiful slow green rivers, pike deep in their weed; hills banked in opening leaves, threaded with ferny paths. Above us, because the car roof was open, the fire-tongued larks spread a light canopy of sound. But of course she didn't hear them.

The Marchesa was still reading her notes when, swinging off on to a byroad I turned to look at those large and practical white hands. Their thumbs were pressed forcefully back against the papers before her like the powerful cocked hammers of a shotgun. She was still reading when I glanced back to the road again and saw, coming fast round the bend, a great lorry high on the crown of the road.

I wasn't frightened. I simply turned the car with a jerk towards the grass verge, just as though it had been a bumper car at a fair. It was almost fun. I could hear my rings clicking against the wheel as I did so. Click and click and click! Quite distinctly.

SIX

For a moment there was total peace. A cool wind was blow-ing. She seemed to be somewhere on a well-known hillside, perhaps on the warm flowery flank of that mountain which rises behind Assisi—Monte Subasio. She could hear the birds singing quite clearly, which should have put her on her guard. There are no birds in Umbria. They shoot them to the last thrush, vigorously, every autumn. She could also hear the sound of a spring rising and falling, running away between stones. In fact the sound of running liquid had all the time been a background to the zephyrous cool and the singing birds, though she'd only just begun to separate it from them. She could hear now that it was a fast, regular splashing, first like tears falling and then like a tap dripping. Then it began falling faster, even faster than the beat of a quick heart, and soon it was falling so fast that it lost its beat altogether and became the hot fluid that she could feel running over her eyes and down her cheek into her neck.

She became conscious of an oddly restricting pressure like thunder coming, like a headache, but not too painful.

She looked up. She stared along a ham-coloured torso and into an odd face. She noted meticulously the brown circular mouth, the great buttock-like cheeks and the protuberant eyes which resolved, when she realised that the man's shirt was torn open to the waist, into his navel, diaphragm and nipples.

In disgust and panic the young man pressed the pad more firmly over the eternally welling crevice in the woman's head, where he could see something white and glutinous that must be the bone of the skull. In his anxiety he pressed too hard and jarred her. Her head turned slackly to one side and she vomited on to the grass, and then choked, unable to clear it.

For a moment she fell into night again, and then air, tainted and used air it seemed, bruise coloured, was trying to break from a stone breast. The man heard trickling whimpers and then something like words. They wouldn't come properly, were only sibilants hissed as though from riddled lungs, breathed up from far down a long grey corridor of some castle-like place where she now lived. The structure itself was barely inhabited, for she'd shrunk so small inside it, to a mere thread indeed, pale and dangling, caught by some mercy on the roughness of the stone coping of a deep dry well, no water in its bottom. She was by now mad with thirst.

He wouldn't let her drink anything, choked back his own nausea and only allowed her to wet her lips from the great cider bottle of soft drink that he had with him in the lorry. It smelt of pear-drops.

She lay there sucking it in, tasting the smell of pear-drops and some other ingredient which was probably blood, and as she did this she began, little by little, to return to that vacated castle. Slowly lights came on. Sputtering flares were lit out and out and out from that central powerhouse of the lungs where for quite a time she'd been skulking, terrified. Lights blazed, one candle taking flame from another in an ecstatic Easter conflagration, along passages, under arches, over crenellated walls to the extremities, to the most distant outposts.

He saw the woman's head turn and her eyes gaze fixedly over the grass as if looking for something. He glanced covertly at his watch, longing for the ambulance to come.

She gazed along the enormous length of the arm which, like Gulliver's, was tacked down by weakness to the glass-scattered summer grass. Drying streamlets of blood still meandered slowly between the knuckles. When she saw the careful shaping of the fingers which she hadn't even identified as her own, she began to weep vaguely at their uselessness. She continued to weep. The leaping candles had already identified where the trouble lay, leaden and unilluminable in the small of the back.

'Back!' she said suddenly, because the man had been trying to prop up her head on his rolled-up coat, but only spent air sighed out between someone else's lips. Sweating, she tried to say it again.

'Lie still, dear!' the young man said. 'There's an ambulance coming. Just lie still!'

She lay for a moment enjoying the peace and lack of pain, and then slowly she began thinking again about the dead place above her bottom. If her back was broken she wouldn't be able to move her feet. She had to know.

So, down the truly immense length of the fallen body she tried guilefully (the young man was smoking and staring up at the sky) to send that so simple order 'Move!' It was more tiring than she'd allowed for, or else the channels, the old channels she'd always used so unthinkingly, were silted up. There was only the painless, completely comfortable in itself—deadness. She waited to try again, furiously impatient in mind. 'Move!'

A long, long time passed. She imagined with hope that the message was moving through alternative labyrinthine systems. Nothing happened. And then, far, far down the line she felt one foot sulkily, but unmistakably, twitch.

They were pulling Belle out, three men. They told me later that the lorry driver hadn't been able to get out of his cab, had just sat there crying because he thought he'd killed us.

It was only when they began pulling Belle out that I suddenly realised that up until now I hadn't given her a thought. I couldn't actually see what was happening because it was on the other side of the car and the men were talking in low voices. Even then it didn't occur to me that Belle might be dead.

At that moment it wouldn't have worried me anyway. The discovery that I could move my foot had filled me with such a strutting sense of almighty power that I could have roused Belle even from death if necessary.

It was this same brassy confidence, this tinny euphoria that enabled me to endure, with ecstasy almost, what came soon; the firm, painful strapping to the stretcher;

the sickly jarring as they lifted and then slid me smoothly into the back of the ambulance; the joyful awaiting, until they should at last slide in, similarly strapped, poor Belle.

When I managed to turn my head and see Belle my first impulse was to laugh. You could see at a glance that poor old Belle was completely unaware of the good news coming to her, of all that power and glory which I possessed and would soon pass on.

She was babbling drowsily, like someone in a deck-chair on a hot afternoon. She was babbling the same thing over and over again. All I could see wrong was a small dark worm of blood issuing from one of her nostrils. That was all.

The ambulance revved, gathered speed. It rocketed along so fast that the busty mutinous nurse who was accompanying us was flung violently back and forth in the gangway between our stretchers. Across this bucking trench I managed slowly to stretch out my hand and hold Belle's. It was warm, but didn't respond when I pressed it.

'What I want to know,' Belle said staring up at the ambulance roof, 'is who was driving?' Her voice was matter-of-fact, a statement rather than a question.

'I was,' I said.

I was quite enjoying this hectic race: the siren blowing, the old ambulance swaying and tossing. There was an exhilarating sense of expedition, of going somewhere after sleep. Life, great life was about to be resumed. I was almost grateful when the ambulance raced up a steep ramp, the daylight went out, and there was a chill antiseptic wind as they opened the door.

·

'Ugh!' said the houseman when he lifted the pad off. The carefully staunched wound opened afresh, voiding blood into her eyes, spattering his white coat. 'Ugh!' He replaced the pad, and then carefully, as though he were dealing with some unwieldy doll, he began articulating with his neat little brown hands her heavy white arms, her legs, weighty as marble. At first he went gently with the legs because she'd complained about her back. 'And that! And that! Good!' he sang when she yelled. 'And that!' when she yelled again.

Now, as though in some opium dream, faces, Asiatic mostly, some of them very beautiful, swung over her like ripe gold fruit exuding ether. Far below her, quite painlessly, drubbed the well-oiled rubber wheels. Soon the drubbing ceased, and she was slid deftly on to hard, cool surfaces. These grew warm beneath her, and, in the gaseous mist of what might or might not have been anaesthetics, concealed machinery hummed and clicked. Then the surface on which she lay suddenly turned hot as blood and out from it sprang a great serrated knife which divided her, shrieking, from herself so that she fainted.

Now the smell of ether grew fainter, wafted away by the fanning of the light perspex doors as they swung open and then shut again. The doors of a mahjong box. Once more I was waiting for aeons upon aeons behind an Oriental screen of green silk. I waited for the singing birds to appear, for I could already hear the covert splash of blood, whether my own or someone else's I wasn't sure. In a few moments more I could hear it quite openly, but didn't say anything about it until they came in, and it was swabbed forcefully away, while, with a sensation as though the birds who had been singing were nimbly stripping and devouring my flesh to the skull, they stitched up my head.

All this time, gaining inexorably on that wholly self-centred though dwindling euphoria, had been the anxious thought of what was happening to Belle.

I tried to ask them. I might have been asking something faintly obscene. They smiled, but didn't answer. Burmese, East Indian and Negro. I only glimpsed through a rent in the green singing-bird screen a trolley being pushed by with someone hiccuping on it. It could have been Belle but I wasn't sure.

'I'm in love,' I suddenly said as we were speeding our way back to the ward, flying along, it seemed, through balsamic air in which the calm Asiatic faces swung like lanterns. 'Are you, dear?' said the nurse. 'That's nice!' and, smiling, she shone the acid beam of her pencil torch deep into my eyes, checking for brain damage.

'Ravished by love!' I went on foolishly.

In the cubicle next to me I could now hear someone talking behind the drawn curtains. They were speaking in the flat matter-of-fact voice which was unmistakably Belle's.

'What I want to know is who was driving? I only hope I wasn't driving.'

'Belle!' I shouted. 'Pull back the curtains, Nurse! It's me, Belle! Nurse, it's my friend!'

'I don't think I should,' said the nurse putting away her torch with a severe expression. And then, 'Oh well, yes!'

'I'm cold,' Belle said, staring up at the ceiling. Blood had dried round her mouth and nose and her hair was rusty with it.

'Oh Belle!' I put out my hand. 'It's Hero here and we're all right.'

'What I want to know,' said Belle turning to me with an extremely severe expression, 'is who was driving? I only hope I wasn't driving.'

'No, I was driving. We came round the corner and there was a lorry coming down the middle of the road and I couldn't stop.'

'Ah!' said Belle apparently taking this in. She was silent for a moment or two and then, severe as before, she said, 'What I want to know is who was driving? I only hope I wasn't driving.' Still retaining her grave expression she began to hiccup.

I slept and day-dreamed and Belle hiccuped most of the hot afternoon. From time to time we were interrupted by staff who came to push hard china spouts between our teeth so that we could suck up tea or cold water. More staff came half-hourly to check for brain damage again with their pencil torches.

In the late afternoon Hugh came with bunches of flowers in cellophane. He went to Belle first. 'What I want to know,' Belle said when he bent over her, 'is who was driving?'

'They're both a little shocked,' explained the nurse.

'Oh!' he said, when he got to my bed. 'They haven't even washed the blood off your hair!'

'Don't worry about that,' I said. 'I'm really quite happy in here.' I was. I was with Belle after all, and I minded no more than she did when he went.

By nightfall Belle, apart from the occasional hiccup, had become completely comatose and wasn't much of a companion. I wasn't feeling so good either. The great muscular rip in my back had expanded into new territories like an occupying army, and there were now only two positions in which I could lie without intense pain. One was if I drew my left knee up to my navel, and the other was when I let it down again. An obsessed piston of flesh, I changed these positions ceaselessly, casting off the bed-covers again and again so that the night-nurse finally became exasperated with picking them up, and gave me a pill. I now passed into a grateful furred darkness for a time, only to wake in muzzy agony because I'd made a false move in my sleep and ricked myself.

Time became never-ending present. I began feebly pistoning once more. For ever and ever, like Tantalus, unable even to stop long enough to hear whether Belle was still breathing or not. The noise I made pistoning under the blankets drowned her faint breath and made me worry in case she'd died. In the muted light of the ward the red blanket over my knees became a mountain gouting blood. I didn't know now whether I would survive the time in which I was living and which was called for no reason I could think of, night.

The nurse came again. This time she was more sympathetic. I'm not sure what she did, or what she gave me, but from that moment the pain and I became one, joined in a love affair that was not, in the end, so very detestable.

Morning came, sunny and blowing, brought by a fat black wardmaid with a cup of tea. I lay still for a time, balancing the feeding-cup on my chest, sucking the hot beautiful stuff through its hard spout, marvelling that the night had actually passed and that Belle and I were still alive.

There was a sudden explosive rattle of curtain rings, the white and blue curtain writhed and danced as a small stocky nurse stood before me with a hot tin bedpan. It was like being back in the school san.

'I'm afraid that I can't do that without help,' I said in a calm voice which concealed my eagerness to make water. I didn't like the thought of a catheter. 'I've hurt my back,' I explained co-operatively.

'Then you'll have to wait, won't you!' yelled the nurse and, swooping round my bed, she dived into Belle's cubicle, tearing the curtain shut behind her.

'Come on, dear!' I heard her say briskly. 'Wake up!'

From behind the curtains came a groan, and then, as the nurse probably attempted to prise up poor Belle's buttocks, horribly, a furious scream.

'I say!' I said, trying to roll over on to my left side to pull back the dividing curtain and tell the nurse about Belle. The inexorable whip slashed across my own buttocks and I collapsed in obedience.

This was the time, I now learned, when day really began, and not at that false dawn of peace when the morning tea was brought in. Now you would have had to block your ears to shut out the moans and groans and choked sighs, the fretful suckings and belchings, the sly, unlocatable tricklings. Every minute or two there was a sharp scream like the sound of a foraging gull, so that the ward seemed not a long room filled with human beings, but a sighing, sobbing sea of anguish.

I was still waiting for my bedpan when they came for Belle. It seemed that yesterday's X-rays were defective and that others would have to be taken. The orderlies getting her on to the trolley were as kind as possible, but with every move they jarred her, and in a way it was a relief when she'd gone. All the time she was away I followed the minutes on my old schoolboy's watch with its bloodstained strap and its plastic face, trying to think of other things and not what might possibly be happening to Belle. In the end, with the sun rising so hot and uncaring outside the windows, sickened by the mingled smells of the lunchtime soup and disinfectant, I submitted to despair.

They brought her back just after twelve. The Burmese nurse who'd gone with her was crying, for which she'd no doubt get a rocket from matron. They drew the curtains round Belle, and a student and two doctors were in there for some time doing something, God knows what, but I could hear resentful hiccups. When they came for me I went with relief, glad to exchange the obscenity of experiencing Belle's pain second-hand for what I prayed would be the bearable rigours of first-hand pains of my own.

We sped gaily almost, Belle's Burmese nurse and I, along the lightsome corridors. When we halted at the small dark lift the temperature suddenly dropped.

I couldn't believe they'd hurt me. It only occurred to me that they might at the door of the dingy-looking X-ray room, where a heavy white girl with blank eyes awaited us. Without looking at me she seized the foot of the bed and with a professional kind of a jerk swivelled it violently round the door jamb. The phone rang as I yelled. When she picked up the receiver, the fat radiologist looked fed-up. It seemed that, unlike Belle's, my pictures had been perfectly okay after all.

Hastily, just in case the fat radiologist changed her mind, the Burmese nurse ran me fleetly up the passage and into the dark lift. Drawing free of that sadistic basement we rumbled back to the ward giggling.

Belle had been asking for me.

In my short absence down at the X-ray department, an indulgent sort of mood had settled on the ward. Perhaps it was because the morning chores were over, or perhaps a new sister had come on duty; I don't know. Anyway, when I asked them they drew back the curtain between Belle and me and pushed our beds together because Belle said she felt like a conversation. But I think they must have given Belle something, because almost at once she disappointingly dozed off and there was a white surgical peace.

'Tell me again what we were doing,' Belle said waking me up with a start. I'd been dreaming about Mrs Shafto's archipelago and was frustrated because I wanted to reach one of the islands and couldn't, because whenever I tried to get into the boat to take me over it shrank so that only my foot could get inside it.

'We'd just come off the A40,' I said and then went over it all again, blow for blow.

'Do you know it's completely gone. I can't remember anything.'

'Don't try.'

'I wasn't driving though?'

'No, I was driving.'

'That's what I wanted to know, who was driving I mean. Hero dear, I suppose we're very lucky to be alive.'

'Yes.'

'Hero, how badly hurt do you think we are?'

'I don't know. The Registrar's coming later. Not all that badly or else we'd be in plaster by now, wouldn't we? What did they say when you went to be X-rayed?'

'I can't remember.'

'Didn't they hurt you?'

'I simply don't remember. I say, you were driving, weren't you?'

'Yes, yes, I was.'

The sun moved round. I made water three times, supported by two kind auxiliaries, one German, one Polish. We had brown bread and butter for tea which was delicious. We dozed again. When we woke the ward was suffused with a tender gold light and the visitors were arriving.

I heard her voice first. It had been unforgettable since that dionysiac evening when Belle and I and the children had thrashed about so irresponsibly in her island plantings. I saw her, made even more portly by the great bunch of flowering cherry that she was carrying, walking down the ward. She gave the flowers to a nurse and sat down on the chair next to Belle's bed and took her hand. She didn't say anything. Once she glanced over Belle towards me, but I kept my eyes closed. Then she began talking in a low voice to Belle, I think about the children, telling Belle they were all right, and Hugh too. Belle didn't remove her hand, which surprised me. Perhaps she was too done in to resist, or perhaps there really was a sort of sympathy between them. Belle might have been killed after all, and there were the children. Mrs Shafto was devoted to them. I had a guilty phantasy that I had been trying to take

Belle away from them and that in that hospital ward her mother-in-law, quietly, but very determinedly, was calling her back to life and duty. Anyway, that's what I thought watching them. Mrs Shafto didn't stay long, but she came over to my bed just before she went and I had to open my eyes, otherwise my lids would have quivered.

'And how do you feel?' I couldn't tell whether she was angry or not. I had, after all, upset her whole family.

'Get better quickly won't you!'

'I will,' I said obediently.

'That's right!' she touched my cheek briefly, but kindly I thought, with her forefinger. Gardening had made it as rough as a nutmeg-grater.

Night came shortly after this, and they parted us, quite suddenly, Belle and me. An emergency had come in who needed the quiet corner I'd been living in, and I was swooped upon by two strange nurses and run to the top of the ward, where an old woman was sitting bolt upright in bed being fed pap by the Italian ward maid. It was terrible, because Belle and I had made our peaceful home in the quiet end and I couldn't bear to think of her going through the night beside someone strange. I began to cry.

The old woman beside me was as deaf as a post and communication was barely possible. Locked in her silence she filled the air with complaints and querulous prayers, only ceasing when, like a strange Cellini grotesque, she was raised on to her bedpan. Then she would yell loudly and briefly before returning to her prayers whilst she did her business. I felt very sorry for her, but, unable either to speak or move, could do nothing, so turned my face to the wall and planned until morning and between bouts of atrocious pain, how I could get back to Belle.

The moment the morning torment was over and the gentle dew, as it had yesterday, settled once more upon the ward, I caught hold of the Burmese nurse as she was speeding past and asked if Belle and I couldn't possibly be pushed together again. She plucked up courage and actually asked the Sister, and the Sister took one look at me, and for some extraordinary reason said yes. The Emergency, who was annoying the nurses because she wouldn't eat anything, was pushed into my place as a punishment, and I was merrily dashed back to Belle in our quiet corner among the white cherry.

'Oh, Hero!' said Belle who'd had a terrible night too. 'Oh, Hero! It's marvellous to see you!' Then, when she was telling me about the awful night and how badly behaved the woman next door had been, we began to laugh. Then we cried, and then we laughed again, even although it hurt our backs every time, until the Burmese nurse came bounding up and said that I'd have to go back beside the old deaf woman immediately if we didn't behave properly.

So we drowsed that day away in our corner of perfect happiness and contentment. But poems have been written about moments like this, so explanation isn't necessary.

Towards lunchtime we became partly aware that in the ward itself some sort of subterranean agitation was going on. The staff, even the few nice ones, seemed tense and snappish, and this, in time, reached the patients.

There'd been a terrible pile-up on the motorway, the black wardmaid said, rolling her eyes. Our beds would have to be cleared for the victims. Someone else said it wasn't a road accident at all, but an explosion at a fire-works factory. Workers had been terribly burned. Belle and I began to worry that we'd be separated again and our happy peace interrupted.

'One of the nurses said we might be here for six weeks,' Belle said. 'Do you think we could get a room in the private wing? You do belong to BUPA don't you?'

'What about your principles?' I asked her.

She smiled. Her bruises made her look like Charles Laughton playing the Hunchback of Notre Dame. Simply hideous.

'Oh, corrupted!' I said.

But in the end there wasn't any need for us to mess about with BUPA or anything else.

The Registrar came after tea. He told us that the submarine swell that we'd been aware of all day actually was something, but not a road or a factory accident. By a strange series of misunderstandings what everyone had taken to be an isolated case of typhoid recorded in the town ten days before had turned out to be not so isolated after all. New cases were coming in fast; beds were in short supply; our injuries, we must realise, though doubtless very painful, were not serious. He would be exceedingly grateful if accommodation could be found for us at home.

They brought us our clothes a short time after this. They hadn't even washed the blood off them and our hair was still stiff with it. When the ambulance men came, the emotional Burmese nurse burst into tears again. When we were carried out into the warm air of the May evening, neither Belle nor I could believe that we'd only been in there forty-eight hours.

SEVEN

'I feel damnably unhappy!'

'Might you be taking yourself a little too seriously?'

'You always try to diminish what I do and feel.'

'Nonsense! You must see that in view of your previous aptitude your present behaviour seems strangely unadaptable.'

'How "adaptable", as you call it, should one be?' Hugh asked.

His mother straightened up from the plant she'd been attending and laughed. To him it was a cruel sound. Exultant. A savage 'Ha! Ha!' among the trumpets.

'Perhaps you were too well organised,' she jeered, 'with your wife and your mistress, altogether too comfortable.' She turned back to her plant, her energetic fingers teak-coloured from crushing and stripping away the sugary infestation of greenfly.

Their bickering was the aftermath of confusion caused by a peremptory ring from the hospital announcing the immediate return of the crash victims. Their return—wounded, bedridden and helpless—was timed to coincide disastrously with the opening of the Rococo Symposium.

For Hugh, disordered by the events of the last week, and indeed for many weeks before that, his mother's offer to accommodate the two invalids had come as an enormous relief. Jessica had already been farmed out with the sympathetic mother of a school-friend.

'You sound as though you're glad,' he persisted, wanting to provoke a row, if only to relax his inner tension. A moderate row yet sufficiently cathartic. He missed Belle.

'Glad!' he repeated.

'I think I am rather glad!'

'Why?'

'Mere pride of sex probably. I don't enjoy seeing my own sex so shamelessly taken advantage of.'

'They like it!'

'So people will tell one. It's perfectly true, of course, that the world was a much less complicated place when everyone thought as you do. I also see there's something very fetching about the idea. I mean the idea of born to rule because of your sex: that whatever you did which affected the minds, bodies and possessions of over half the world's population was not only natural but right. I think if I'd been a man I'd have liked that too.'

'Some women do like it,' he insisted. 'Being exploited. You don't, but the really feminine ones do.'

'Very possibly,' said his mother. 'I suppose it's a form of despair—liking it. Though sometimes I feel frightened when I think of what horrors may fill the vacuum created by the cynicism of people like you!'

'It's not cynicism, it's anthropology!'

'I know, I know. You'll tell me, very broadly speaking, that there are two kinds of women: the matriarchal ones who, in a male-dominated society, become militant and noisy out of frustration, and the vulnerable, raped captives who either keep quiet or become nags!'

'Which are you?'

'Guess!'

'. . . though sexual tyranny has nothing on the tyranny of parenthood,' said Hugh, nimbly changing tack. 'One can't even hit one's mother because there's some ridiculously unfair inbuilt taboo which prevents it. Mother and son! My God!'

She laughed again. 'It's really a clashing of jealousies. You are annoyed that I gave you the day as the French say, and I must agree that it is annoying to be made, created, without one's permission . . .'

'. . . and you are annoyed that you aren't a man?'

'No! No! you're wrong there. I'm much more like the calamitous wife of the poor fisherman in the fairy story. I don't wish that I'd been born a man, I wish I'd been God!'

'Do you think you would have made a good job of it?'

'I'd like you to tell me. Would I?'

'That's something I simply couldn't answer.'

'Try!'

He looked down at her with amusement and diminishing hatred. Stocky, defeatingly energetic, she stared back at him undaunted, her sherry-coloured Celtic eyes smiling and insolent.

'Oh to be God!' he cried, and bent to kiss her and make peace. He implied a disgusted criticism of a world in which chance prevailed—chance making you miss trains or catch them; chance locking up people until death in inadequately-functioning, wrongly-coloured, wrongly-sexed bodies. Ariels shut in trees.

'A world of basic insolubles,' he said. 'Like you and me!' he added demurely, to tease her.

'Come, come!'

'There is always the possibility of reconciliation, of course? Of resolution?'

'Of course! Remembering too that the daily sustaining of the creation may be as creative as the creation itself . . .'

'. . . and that outside us, though perhaps not all that interested in us personally . . .'

'Not at all interested in us,' added Mrs Shafto.

'. . . an ideal state of affairs prevails where all has long been reconciled. Remote it is, unattainable certainly in this life . . .'

'. . . but nevertheless,' she finished for him and laughed, 'reminding us always . . .'

They were interrupted by a heavy vehicle drubbing over the railway-sleepers which paved the causeway to Mrs Shafto's farm.

'Oh God!' said Hugh, 'I think it's the ambulance.'

For a moment neither of them was willing to make the necessary move. Encapsulated in late afternoon heat, they had both been experiencing a refreshing time-arrest, during which, like fish in a tank, they had swum close to re-experience each other's known, if not particularly loved or venerated, spiritual contours. Hugh at least had been reassured.

Now change awaited them, shut up and mute as yet, inside the white hearse-like vehicle with blacked-out windows. From it two uniformed men were now smartly jumping down.

It's like the arrival of the baker's van, thought Hugh, and the image was given further substance when he and his mother, gaining the ambulance, peered into its rear compartment where, blinking owlishly in the sunlight, his wife and mistress lay beneath warm crimson blankets waiting to be pulled out on stretchers.

Mrs Shafto stared at them with muted compassion.

'It's sickening to be so harassed by the imprudent marriages of one's children,' she'd said to Hugh earlier in the day. 'And their affairs,' she'd added.

Her daughter-in-law irritated her extremely, though by and large she acknowledged that Belle had probably been good for Hugh, if only in the restricted sense that medicine can be good. Compound frequently fall in love with simple natures. Mrs Shafto had not fallen in love with Belle. The clear, direct, and to her ineffably limited personality of her grandchildren's mother gritted even upon her strong nerves. There were no interesting corners in Belle's nature for Mrs Shafto to dwell on or explore (Hugh had not told her about the Irish horses, which might have made a slight difference), for it was a nature which drew upon a view of life utterly mechanistic and casual. In her mother-in-law's imagination, Belle's nature was smooth and antiseptic, a flat white statement, as alien and inarguable with as a toilet pedestal.

She greeted the arrival of Hero with equally little pleasure. Here the matriarch in her would have already sensed danger even if she had not been apprised of the messy, and to her boring, *ménage à trois* that Hero's presence had created.

'And now it looks as though Belle's falling in love with her!' Hugh had wailed, while at the water's edge Mrs Shafto's glossy rowing-boat leaped and tugged like a hooked trout, longing, it would appear, as she did herself, to leave immediately for the islands, where among the wide-opened leaves of her trees, the birds, unlike humans, were rearing their young so neatly and responsibly.

'Nonsense! I've never heard of anything so absurd!'

'It's true!'

'Well, then, you must have been a very selfish husband to drive her to that!'

'Belle was exceedingly happy. Everyone was happy. It was all working so well.'

'It had no business to work well. I wish you wouldn't tell me such things.'

'I wish I didn't have to,' he said, wallowing haplessly in hideous misery and dependence.

'My age should protect me from this sort of revelation,' she said. 'It's the expected result of barbarous behaviour. Modern behaviour. Unnatural behaviour. Once you begin living irregularly all else . . .'

'. . . follows! I know, I know! You don't need to tell me!'

'I'll have them here,' she'd said ungraciously, 'though I don't want to,' resolving that if she could she would laugh them out of their obsession somehow. Stupid, idle women! Anything to bring about peace and to ensure that her grandchildren didn't suffer. Unlike her own children, her grandchildren must be protected.

By now her unwanted guests were being ponderously manoeuvred into the house, to the accompaniment of bawled instructions from the ambulance men. Should I tip them? she wondered, and then, how long will they have to stay, she asked herself, desiring already to be rid of them.

Life in the last six years had become more full, content, and, the only word she could think of to describe it was 'proportionate', than she'd ever imagined possible again. In her small kingdom here there had been a resolution of all that had once nettled and upset her. She had begun, or felt she had begun to unlearn at last that bad lesson unhappily taught so long ago in India. Here among her waters and her planted islands she had been able for the first time to regard herself with equanimity. Why not?

> Paradise, and groves
> Elysian, Fortunate Fields—like those of old
> Sought in the Atlantic Main—why should they be
> A history only of departed things
> Or a mere fiction of what never was?

Or so she told herself.

Disturbed, she followed, unwillingly, the cortège into the house, pausing for some minutes in her drawing-room while she waited for the sounds of movement to subside in the room above. She had assigned a double room to her two guests in the sour hope that propinquity would produce boredom, and that, soon tiring of one another, they would part and harmony be restored within the family.

The drawing-room windows were only a few yards from the grassy brink of the water-filled gravel pit, so that when the sun shone its beams flashed restlessly off the moving waters of Mrs Shafto's inland sea, covering the walls and ceilings of the room with playing light as though on the walls of an Atlantic cave. For a time she stood there stolid among the mercurial lights, staring absently at the headlines of the evening paper which lay on the chair arm. 80 CONFIRMED CASES. It meant nothing to her.

Upstairs, her visitors, if you could call them that, left alone at last by ambulance men, lover and husband, lay silent, exhausted. The same water-reflections playing through their windows caressed, hypnotically, their tired eyes, while their ears, accustomed to the din of the ward, were soothed by the fast lapping waves of the archipelago. When Mrs Shafto put her head round their bedroom door ten minutes later, they were both, thankfully, asleep.

Two days later, the Rococo Symposium began. Sifting the grain from the chaff as the new arrivals strolled about in the warm green shade beneath the Beaudesert limes, Hugh was a little disappointed to see that those attending were neither quite so numerous nor so totally representative as he'd feared. He reflected that on the whole this was unsurprising, for the Rococo is not everyone's cup of tea, being apt to inspire either neurotic infatuation or violent revulsion rather than that even admiration excited by less controversial styles. Morally, indeed, on nearly every count, the Rococo was indefensible. This was of course why Hugh had chosen it. In the first place it was the style favoured by the most outrageous people—Louis Quinze, Frederick the Great and impossible Catherine, for a start. It had been paid for in the blood and wounds of those least able to bear such burdens. It was a style artificial in the highest degree, presupposing in the spectator (and here was the rub) a cultivated and prepared state of mind, a cynical mind, implying élitism and aristocracy. It was also the style of phantasy and escape, of shutting out disagreeable reality. It was the style of impertinence and irresponsibility, of effeminate giggles, of prurience and pointless, undeserved leisure. It was the style of whipped-cream bums; nipples like glacé cherries; cocks of peppermint; cunts of crystallised rose petals. It was without question the worst and most provocative of all styles.

By teatime, served where the Beaudesert servants had once eaten, in a depressing, dark-panelled hall ornamented with colossal stuffed fish and the showy parts of slaughtered elephant and rhinoceros, Hugh had picked out from his thirty-odd guests the two who were most likely to give trouble.

Needless to say, neither of them absolutely fell into the simple category of Rococo idolator or Rococo detestor. Dr Chieseman could, at a pinch, be designated the lover, though his love was a tormented, incommunicable, inward-bleeding thing. Watching him walking apart from the others, deliberately, it seemed, seeking out the dampest and most solitary paths to remote urns and ponds, Hugh felt a certain sympathy with him, though he sensed that Dr Chieseman was the kind of man who would take a perverse pleasure in disagreement, possibly to the point even of disrupting Hugh's seminars. He would dismiss, Hugh was sure, the essential fun aspect of the Rococo, and would try to trap Hugh into listening to endless dissertations upon cabinet-makers whose work Hugh had never seen and remote porcelain factories he'd never heard of. Mrs Crosroyde on the other hand would delight in the sociological aspect; indeed, Mrs Crosroyde striding around the house and grounds was a kind of rape. Why people like Mrs Crosroyde should attend a Symposium of this sort he couldn't imagine, but from experience Hugh had found out that they always, always did. From the moment she opened her mouth, Hugh prophesied long wrangles about poor Madame de Pompadour's venality and sensuality, only minimally forgiven because she had provided work for the starving by establishing the ceramics factory at Vincennes.

His prognostication was amply confirmed later that evening when, badly missing Belle and Hero, he was moving among his unwanted guests at the introductory sherry party he'd arranged, and came upon the Chieseman and the Crosroyde already crossing swords.

'As you know, when she died the inventory of her possessions filled two hundred quarto pages and took two notaries a year to make!' The shortcomings, as Hugh had foretold, of the unfortunate de Pompadour. Dr Chieseman, with a mouth closed and pink as a cat's anus, was staring straight in front of him, and only looked a fraction less disagreeable when Hugh stopped beside them. He then asked whether Hugh's lectures were to cover aspects of the German Rococo and in particular the work of Cuvilliès, and if not why not?

'You must meet my secretary!' cried Hugh treacherously, signalling Rosa over, and he left them, the Doctor standing impervious apparently to Rosa's pretty enthusiasm while he lectured both her and Mrs Crosroyde as well on the arabesques at Amalienburg.

Although he had been correct in his assumptions about Chieseman and Crosroyde, Hugh had been mistaken in assuming a middle-class uniformity about the rest of the group. Wandering among them he discovered that there were quite enough common voices among the remainder of his guests to convince him that Beaudesert had, after all, been truly breached by the advance guard of that alien and threatening class which would one day destroy everything he held most dear. How, he wondered, was he going to make contact with them over the hapless, hopeless gaiety of Rococo chairs, for instance? Chaises en gerbe, en lyre, en éventail, chaises voyeuses, chaises d'affaires, chaises bidets? What about the beds? Paphoses, turquoises, duchesses, duchesses brisées, sultanes, ottomanes . . . it was impossible. All these things seemed, studying their serious faces, irrelevant in the extreme, and he had been a fool to choose such a subject.

He felt suddenly the true and crushing weight of what had happened, felt sick, imagining, in the closing night, Rosa down at the main entrance testing the alarm bells, checking the guards, for God's sake locking him *in* with the Enemy.

Thankfully the party was thinning, people returning to their rooms before partaking of the terrible cafeteria meal which, Hugh knew, awaited them. Still stuck with Dr Chieseman, Rosa was now gesticulating passionately. She appeared to be making some impression upon the Doctor because he was listening to her, but whether favourably or not it was hard to discern. Mrs Crosroyde had gone. He felt himself longing again for Belle, for Hero, and then felt a surge of jealousy at the mere thought of them down there at his mother's, at that place which for fun, in contradistinction to his Beaudesert Versailles, he had jokingly called Marly. Marly where it never rained. Out of the racket. Out of reach. As he calmly wished good-night to the dreadful people filing past him he reflected that in three months he had lost undisputed possession of his mistress, probably of his wife and now of his collection.

The last guest gone, even Rosa, even the haunting Chieseman who had left with her, he picked up the evening paper and saw, glancing through it, that the inconvenient typhoid outbreak which had so untimely driven Belle and Hero from the hospital, had now risen to ninety-seven confirmed cases. The source had now been disclosed as a tin of corned beef. It seemed that the tainted meat had contaminated the slicing machine, which in its turn had affected the other meats it had dealt with in the course of the day. Decay and disaffection everywhere he thought gloomily, and pouring himself another drink wondered how soon he could decently telephone his mother again to ask about the invalids.

At about this time, while a white moon had moved into the sky and an owl was whickering softly in the trees by the water, I was reading Donne. It seemed so apposite to my case:

> But of our dallyance no more signes there are
> Than fishes leave in streams or Birds in aire
> And betweene us all sweetness may be had
> All, all that Nature yields or Art can add.

Admittedly there had not been much dalliance. Unless you could count several scenes of an affectionate though eccentric kind in the hospital, but from this promising though semi-concussed condition Belle had by now almost recovered.

We were lying flat upon our beds, but by now were no longer so absolutely bound to them as two days ago, because frequently, like two crazy drunks, we had encouraged one another to squirm off our mattresses and claw our way to the lav at the end of the passage. Apart from spending hour after hour together in the same room, there could now have been very little private between us. Each of us had taken turns to hang over the other at the ready with sticks and rolls of toilet paper, as they sat on the W.C., an absolute necessity when one false turn of the torso could cause a moment of agony so commanding that one all but fainted.

'What are you reading? It's getting too dark to see,' Belle complained.

'I'm reading poetry.'

I seemed to have been reading poetry for aeons in the light-washed shell of our bedroom, our Atlantic cave, webbed with the light that the sun struck off the waves outside. I had gorged myself on verse (what other food was there?) while Belle, between bouts of eating and sleeping, had been writing out a sort of report about certain unsatisfactory aspects of our treatment in hospital. She now laid her file aside and said, 'Read me some poetry!'

So, as the room darkened I read her the whole of 'Sappho to Philaenis', or nearly the whole of it:

Me, in my glasse, I call thee, But alas
When I would kisse, teares dimme mine eyes and glasse
O cure this loving madness, and restore
Me to mee; thee, my halfe, my all, my more.

I don't think it's a particularly good poem, but when I came
to this I couldn't go on because I was crying. A lot of it was
probably shock that I hadn't got over; also my nights had
been restless, and deep inside me, but without my locating
it, there was an area where I didn't feel frightfully well.

Belle was quite silent, and then I said, 'Darling Belle,
I love you!'

'I know.'

At that the air of our room, our shell, our cave, call
it what you like, seemed to be swarming with the sweet
stingless sound of homecoming bees, and this furred, gold
song sang in my ears and in my eyes and nostrils.

'Come here!' Belle said and put out her hand. Obediently and, for a wonder, quite painlessly, I rolled from my
bed and went to her. She gently drew me down beside
her and I lay on the outside cover, my cheek against hers.
Then I gave her my hand, and absently or so it seemed, or
perhaps from long habit, she laid it against her breast, a
breast so soft, so unimaginably soft that, as the Scriptures
tell us, it was like a heap of fine-dredged flour.

'When did you know?' I asked, and the delicate beating of those thousand wings turned, within my breast, to
warm gold rain.

'The one thing you must hold on to is that it's quite
normal,' Belle said. 'It doesn't shock or surprise me in
the least, and I don't want you to worry either,' and she

squeezed my inert hand against her. 'We're all ambivalent in some way or another, but of course you knew that!'

The warm rain, the high burnished humming ceased, and I could hear properly once more. I could hear Belle's even breathing mingling with my short terrier-like pants, and in what would have been called the 'owl light' from the window I could just see the shaded irregular mound of her bruised forehead.

'I mean one is amazed,' said Belle, 'at the really terribly vague demarcation line there is between what's male and what's female. For instance, did you know what a negative function that Y-chromosome actually has? Did you know that when a Y-carrying sperm fertilises an ovum it simply *reduces* the amount of *femaleness* which would have resulted in the formation of a female foetus? Ssh!' said Belle in the silence which followed this revelation. 'Just be!'

Was this a covert invitation to a licence I had never dreamed of? Could it be that I might now not only fill my hand (which was actually beginning to ache quite badly) with the floweringness of Belle's angel breast, but also kiss into softness those grave and beautiful lips? Might I perhaps take, only God knew what, other liberties? I was not sure.

'The best thing is to talk about it,' said Belle.

'I want to! Oh, I do want to!'

'Not put any obstacles in the way,' continued Belle, promisingly.

'Of course not, of course not!'

'I personally think that there are many, many lost or forgotten relationships,' said Belle, 'and that what we nowadays associate with a purely sexual relationship once also played a part in relationships that weren't specifically sexual. I mean, for a start at one time everyone used to sleep in double beds, didn't they?'

Lovely, lovely time! But was she being subtle or really a bit obtuse? Again I wasn't sure.

'You see I don't happen to think there's any harm in two friends sleeping together for company,' said Belle, 'or hugging each other, or even kissing each other.'

'What would there be harm in, do you think?' I asked. I felt pretty sure that what I had so strangely come to feel for Belle would be very likely—alas—to fall into the category of what she might call 'harm'.

'What would there be harm in?' repeated Belle. 'Well, I don't honestly know. I think it would be something you'd just know inside yourself, just "harm".'

'Dear Belle!' I said, and turned my head and kissed her cheek, and in doing so ricked my back. She smiled. I could see the moonlight on her strong beautiful teeth as she lay there mysteriously smiling. Simonetta Vespucci.

We lay side by side in silence for some moments. Nothing happened. Nothing from Belle's end. I was growing painfully stiff. Cautiously I moved my aching hand that was underneath Belle's, hoping without offence to free it. Instantly she pressed it closer to her. It soon became something not my own. A painful wanting-to-moan root. A bloodless, racked stick held aloft for penance by a holy man on a board of nails. Still Belle said nothing. Lying there beside her I pondered in anguish at the so unfair discrepancy between phantasy and actuality. How often had I dreamed of being here! Risking another rick I turned my head and looked at her. Her eyes were wide open. There were morsels of liquid moonlight between their parian lids.

'I think,' she said at last, 'I think we should help each other to get up. Hugh's mother so hates dinner to be kept waiting.'

It was to be the same both that night, and for the two succeeding nights when Belle, presumably in the interests of therapeutics, once more invited me to lie with her if I would. The moving undertones that this beautiful phrase suggests were in fact no accurate picture of what actually took place.

'Don't be afraid,' Belle said on the second night. 'I feel you're holding back in some way. Touch me. Touch me anywhere if you want to. Don't stop yourself doing anything. It's the only way.'

This time I laid my hand hesitantly over her firm stomach. Some intricate digestive process vibrated delicately, and it seemed queryingly, below my fingers. I stroked my way gently down over her stomach to the tops of Belle's thighs. She parted them instantly, talking all the time.

'Not long ago I met someone who'd been a wardress at Aylesbury prison, and . . .'

Was she really terribly clever? Her body was quite, quite cool. Mine burning. All night, when I returned to my own bed, I was unable to sleep a wink because of restlessness and a queer kind of nausea.

Mrs Shafto played it very oblique all this time, very oblique indeed. Possibly, I accorded to her powers that she didn't really possess, because even in the daytime my love-sickness was making me feel so really ill. But I imagined that her dark quizzical eyes saw everything and mocked it. I don't know. She gardened most of the day, dressed up, in spite of the heat, like some medieval peasant in breeches and a shirt covered by a fustian apron. From where I lolled, sweating out the placid burning hours, I could see her moving serenely through her herbaceous borders, her head screened from the crackling June heat by an enormous straw hat. And while Belle lay sunbathing unconcernedly at the water's edge, Mrs Shafto sometimes came down to fish by us and I'd lie there, my mind filled with feverish and uninnocent longings, while she dexterously caught great gold chub with ruby eyes. Once she'd hooked them, she'd free them and put them in a keep net.

Hugh came twice while we were there, but his presence, poor Hughie—and how could he help it?—produced discordancy. But he was elegant and funny about the Symposium, now in its third unrepeatable day. It seemed likely, he told us, that it would be cut short because people were getting the wind up about the typhoid outbreak. 136 confirmed cases, had we read? There were now over a thousand contacts. They thought it had been started by one renegade tin from a consignment of beef that had been imported thirteen years before and stored in funkholes in case of an H-bomb attack. They'd closed all the Beaudesert schools, and a maternity home on the outskirts of the town had been evacuated to take the victims. To me however, lying there, love-racked and enfeebled, sipping Julia's home-made lemonade, gazing into the flowery grass of the islands in the Archipelago, waiting for the night, the news was unimportant.

Hugh kissed us both and went, and I was glad that he didn't stay. The interlude before bed was usually the best part of the day and I preferred to enjoy Belle and her mother-in-law alone.

Mrs Shafto conversed socratically, in questions. I didn't mind. It was a welcome pedantry for me who, after living so long with men, was used to being told rather than asked things. I think Belle liked it, too. Mrs Shafto had now been told about the Irish horses; enlightened over the Abortion Law, heard criticism of the Tridentine Mass; been advised to read *The Divided Self* and *One Dimensional Man*, though hadn't. They had also discussed, sensibly, India. This evening, however, when it came at last was a disappointment.

'You've been too much in the sun,' Belle said.

'It reflects from the water,' said Mrs Shafto, and gave me a sharp glance. I could see the flames from the candles flickering in her black pupils.

I couldn't eat. But I was content to sit and listen to Belle and Kate Shafto amiably bickering over the candles. I drank three glasses of wine and ate some grapes. Then I went up to bed early and lay waiting for Belle and listening to the soporific slapping of the water against the shore.

She woke me up by sitting heavily on the bed. 'Darling, how hot you are!' She had her cool hands on my wrists.

Half-aware, I put my arms round her neck and drew her face down to mine. There was a small hesitation and then quite suddenly, which she had never done before, she kissed me. On the mouth.

It was a great victory. It was a great defeat. I had hardly been able to take in this tumult of joy when I realised that we were now joining in a kind of strange and ungainly battle. We wrestled rather aimlessly for a moment, now this way, now that, the moon spinning dizzily, sometimes pear-, sometimes apple-shaped, through the old uneven bottle-glass of the windows. Then suddenly, without warning Belle stopped yawing about and stood up, leaving a kind of cooling brutal tear where she'd lain along my side.

'You're ill, darling!' she was saying like someone in a silly Hollywood film, and I thought how unfair because she'd been making just as much of a fool of herself as I had. 'Hero, you must stop, you're dreadfully, dreadfully ill!'

EIGHT

They made a place for me in the old red-brick fever-hospital on the outskirts of the town. There I lay with a high temperature, racked with flying pains in my belly, counting, as in a monochrome nightmare, the geometric tiles lining what I think must once have been a sluice, for there were peeling disconnected pipes protruding from both floor and ceiling. Meanwhile they drew blood and faeces from me in which to grow the suspect bacilli. Looking back, I think this was unnecessary, for I must have been a typical case from the outset, my body sliding about in a caul of sweat and turning out, as though it had been a great kitchen, noisome bouillons from almost every orifice, while over my thighs and neat unstretched belly appeared, even as I stared, a teeming host of salmon-coloured spots.

The name of what I had was a deceitful euphemism for the actuality. To the uninitiated, Phage 34 sounds ordered, shapely, antiseptic even. In reality it is the name of a rioting brute that spawns in warm faeces and rotting meat. A terrible reminder, or so it was to me, of the too-close relation of mouth and anus; a revelation of our true nature, which is that we are great worms gorging at one end objects so shapely and beautiful as leaves and fruits and grasses and swimming fish, only to discharge them, putrescent and shapeless, over the night-stool at the other. *S. typhi* can be transferred only in one way they believe; not by breath nor touch, but by the commerce of filthy hands. From anus, to hand, to mouth.

I could escape, to some extent, the obsession with this loathsome nature of my infection, at night, for at night, between bouts of sleeplessness when I awoke crying because it was only a dream, I possessed Belle.

It was a strange possession. At first I had to escape from where I was. They'd double-locked the white, panelled doors of the sluice and someone had driven six-inch nails obliquely into the door through the jambs, though they must have known as they did it that the wood wasn't all that strong, and that if I crashed myself again and again against the door, the cheap lock would give, the puny bolt bend, while by twisting the nails this way and that I could finally tear them out with my fingers, passion having made them as relentlessly gripping and careless of self-injury as steel pincers. But when I got out at last and, travelling by ways that I can no longer remember except that they were bleak, sunless, airless, exhausting, and reached where I knew Belle was, I'd find only a tree. I can't say what kind of tree, but it was as tall as a swamp cypress, and like a swamp cypress it had its roots in water that flowed clear and mild, halfway up its trunk. But its bark was as smooth as bone, and my arms could just meet around its trunk, and standing in the water I could look up into its top branches where its leaves, broad and thin as those of runner-bean leaves, flourished, full of birds, in the sunshine far above my head. I could, if I stretched, run my hands down its lower branches and smooth my fingers round the beautiful chalices where they met the main trunk. Sometimes I felt water there. From rain? Or had perhaps the river risen in the night and left its waves there? When I sucked my fingers afterwards they tasted faintly sweet. I could also, without having to hold my breath, dip my head beneath the water and, closing my eyes, trace that portion of the lower trunk which grew so strangely there. It was as smooth as the upper portion, save where it divided into the great roots which anchored it in the substratum of the lagoon. Here a species of weed grew, soft as moss, and when I opened my eyes to look at it I could see that it was dark green, and that when I stroked it, it released a stream of minute oxygen bubbles into the surrounding water, and when I took it between my lips and tasted it, it was slightly fizzy on the tongue, like pétillant wine. I soon found, on gently pressing my fingers through the silky weed, that it was concealing a small cave, smooth and arched. The wood of this part of the tree seemed softer than that of the rest, and capable of expansion and contraction. I found this out because there were times when the cavity would only just admit my hand, whilst at others I could get first my head, and then, with gentle pressure, the whole of myself inside. Here I could lie whole hours, perfectly at peace, and in a kind of warmth. I think the small cave was probably off the main current so that the sunlight above, presumably passing through the tree's leaves and conducted down its trunk and into its roots, had time to heat the unstirring water. Lying here I could see, through the cleft by which I had come in, the faster water moving past. Sometimes there were fallen leaves in it, spinning slowly round in the current, sometimes white flower petals; sometimes there were fish poised against the current, as motionless as a kestrel in the air. I used to rest my five wits in the cave, becoming only an ear listening to the minute searching water-currents as with gentle insistence they explored roots and stones and eddied round the whiskers of the waiting chub with the red eyes; or I became only a tongue, softly exploring the smooth salt-tasting walls of the cave until I happened on little wood-knots which, if gently probed, opened suddenly releasing intense sweetness . . . When I awoke from this dream I was always crying. I cried because the dream had turned out to be only a dream, and because I knew I would never survive the hideous day that followed, when I'd lie in bed multiplying, dividing, subtracting the sluice tiles.

It may have been the fever which the ampicillin they were giving me hadn't yet brought down, but I was unable to eat. Everything they put in front of me seemed already dung, and not worth the trouble of my further converting. In the end the only cleanness seemed to be death, and the opting out of life into it the only rational answer. I could see, lying there, that it was all indeed a white lie, a shining stink, the clean glazed tiles of the sluice, the glittering white crockery, used only by me, as indeed was the stainless and burnished bedpan. Inhabiting this antiseptic desert was I, a great sack, a great rotting fruit within which moved a stranger's seed that had been warmed and nurtured in a foreign gut. A vile implantation. An outrage. An atrocious soft rape.

On the fourth day, mad with self-disgust, longing for sleep or death, my throat closed up in protest and I couldn't swallow.

They sent for a psychiatrist, because even if you've got Phage 34 you can be visited. There is, after all, as I've said, only one way of catching the thing, though for form's sake your visitors have to wear gowns and masks.

Dr Rabbinovitz was a kind, fat man with grey mystic's eyes, very gentle. He didn't bother about wearing the mask, knowing as well as I did how the thing is caught, just pushed it up and smiled as soon as the nurse had gone out of the room. He came every day for an hour and simply told me to talk, and if I couldn't talk he just went away and left me in peace to count tiles.

'Talk!' he said. 'Just talk!' So I did, though to begin with I had to keep spitting saliva into my handkerchief because I couldn't swallow it, but he paid no attention to this, only stared up at the clouds sailing past the high-barred window, and waited.

I talked to him about everything that came into my head. To begin with it was mostly fringe matters, irrelevancies, the kind of day it was and what it reminded me of, things like that. Then gradually these isolated fragments, these apparent irrelevancies, began to assume what I took to be some sort of pattern, like iron filings grouping and coalescing about the as yet unknown but magnetic central point. That's what seemed to happen anyway. And as I talked and he so patiently listened, there began to develop what I can only call a sense of

loss. Stronger and stronger. A sense of appallingly posi-
tive loss. But a loss of what, I wasn't yet sure. I told him
about things that had always lingered in my memory,
things that had worried me, if only vaguely, because
of the feeling afterwards; like the time I gazed into a
thrush's nest and then systematically broke every egg it
contained, and then wished I hadn't; and the time that,
searching for wild strawberries on a leafy bank, I dropped
one and couldn't ever find it again and minded about it,
even though there were hundreds of others I could have
had anyway. Then I wound up with the worst dream I'd
ever had which was of my mother, who'd been beautiful,
swinging round, with what I'd always thought of as her
'foxtrot smile', impaled through the navel on a meathook.
I'd once found a sketch of exactly what I'd dreamed in
one of Jung's huge volumes, but had had to leave the
bookshop in a hurry for some reason, never having time
to read the explanation or even to take the page number.
Loss again.

After a number of Dr Rabbinovitz's visits I didn't need
to spit out my saliva quite so much, and I could tell him
how people had worried a good deal about me not crying
when I heard that the Japs had killed my mother and father
in Borneo. Much later I found out that my father's head
had been sliced clean off by a panga. I never tried to find
out how my mother had died because I was pretty sure
that I already knew.

I told Dr Rabbinovitz that I now realised that my parents' deaths hadn't upset me as much as they might because
I could now see that even then, young as I was, I had a deep
sense of their treachery at sailing away P and O and leaving

me behind in England, even although I was exceedingly, though shallowly happy with Auntie Do who was very kind to me. Then at last I came back to everything that had happened in the last few months, and I said to Dr Rabbinovitz that I must have been bottling up the significant hook dream and that great love-hate thing which I'd had for my mother, and for some reason that I didn't yet fully understand, I'd released it all on to poor Belle. For whatever people bleat about love, I told Dr Rabbinovitz, love is first and foremost need, and underneath all the cover up of successful affairs with men and whoopee orgasms etc., everything, everything, I had really been needing my mother. Now, having found her in Belle, I had got to do without her. And this, I told Dr Rabbinovitz, when you really considered it, was learning to do without heaven from which I imagined we all came, Mother being the last outpost of that beautiful, tormenting, never wholly forgotten region which we seek for again and again in sex—and sometimes, in death.

Unfortunately, though this explanation was quite satisfactory both to Dr Rabbinovitz and to me, this wasn't the end of it. While I'd been lying there in the sluice something else had begun to worry me terribly, and this was determinism, and I had to tell poor Doctor R. about that too. I told him inexorably about those exterior events, so apparently nothing to do with me, which had yet turned out to be so important that it made my breath catch in terror at the machine-like working of our universe.

I mean that eleven months back when I was being Hughie's most happy and contented mistress, in that

very July when we'd learned to make love so well, a small
Dutch freighter had docked at Wapping with a cargo of
rice, sheepskins and 2,016 cans of corned beef. The cans
of corned beef were apparently stinking, and the dockers,
who were on piecework, sorted the good from the bad as
well as they could, and, quite rightly I think, demanded
extra money for it. They must have done this work extraordinarily well, because of the remaining 1,500 cans that
were then redistributed and sent out to all four corners of
the kingdom, only one was contaminated.

I have since learned that corned-beef cans are made
like boxes with the lid off. The beef is boiled, drained
and forced into the tins, then the top is sealed but for a
small hole from which all the air inside the tin is sucked
out by an extractor. This small hole is then sealed by a
'brogue' tongue which is soldered. After that it is really
only a million to one that that tin can be penetrated by
anything. Yet, while in that early summer Hugh and I
lay in one another's arms and I was rebinding *Tristram
Shandy* for him, there was one tin cooling in the river
which ran past the El Durazill cannery in Cordoba.
A poor workman from the camp further up river used
the river as there were no proper toilet facilities at the
camp, and the bacilli from him washed down the river
and found its way into the can by way of the badly-
soldered 'brogue'.

This was in April. By April of the following year meat
from the contaminated tin was being sliced in our new
Beaudesert supermarket. By May 21st, fourteen people
had typhoid. A week later there were 102 cases and 1,000
contacts. By the time I'd got to the sluice in the old fever

hospital, 224 cases, 2,500 contacts. I must have eaten some of the meat in a sandwich before I'd even met Belle; must have been incubating the bacilli whilst I was falling in love. It had finally shown itself the night I found that in spite of herself Belle perhaps also loved me. It had been my holy present to her. I wondered, I said to Dr Rabbinovitz, whether or not God was behind it all?

Although I wasn't able to answer this particular question to our satisfaction, by the 10th of the month, when I'd completed the story of my life, considered, and satisfactorily explained it to myself and Dr Rabbinovitz, my gullet, mysteriously, like Zacharias's, opened and I could swallow again.

Dear Dr Rabbinovitz congratulated me, implacably refused to give me any advice for my future, went away, and did not return. But he said I should see visitors.

By then I was feeling much better. My spots had faded and so had my phantasies, luckily also my disgust at eating. So that when someone in a voluminous green boorka and mask appeared at my bedroom door and turned out, beneath this disguise, to be Mrs Shafto, I think even she was surprised by my cheerful appearance.

'I don't think you really need wear the mask,' I said. 'It's honestly only a formality.'

'Really not necessary? Thank God! This room is frightfully overheated.' She put an earthenware bowl full of wet white pebbles down on the table. White shoots like pressed snow were spearing up through the pebbles. 'Autumn crocuses!' she said.

'This thing's not caught through the breath,' I persisted, 'only through contact with the faeces.'

'Well, that's not very likely is it?' She removed her mask and sat down heavily.

'It was nice of you to come,' I said. I lay looking at her, thinking how huge she bulked in this small room; how unfamiliar, how vital. But then I had seen no one from the outside except the nurses and Dr Rabbinovitz.

'They declare that this is destiny day,' she was saying. Her eyes in their deep bone caves shaded with tired violet were bright as sea anemones, their lids heavy and white, too heavy to raise this afternoon except in animosity or perhaps in malicious laughter. 'If there's an increase of thirty or more cases tonight, there's a third wave on the way, and that could mean a national disaster, a true plague of Egypt. It seems so unbelievable in all this beautiful weather that there should be germs absolutely everywhere!'

'What about Belle?' I asked. I couldn't help it.

'I'm afraid Belle's gone,' said Mrs Shafto, 'and taken my dear youngest grandchild with her.'

'I'm so sorry,' I said.

'Are you?'

I think I had known all this time that Belle had gone. It also had something to do with my being struck not exactly dumb, but unable to swallow. I suppose Hugh's mother knew all as they say. I wondered, though, if it had been Hugh who'd told her.

'How did it happen?'

'There was an éclaircissement between Hugh and Belle. Belle didn't take it very well.'

'An éclaircissement about Hugh and me, you mean?'

'I imagine so.'

'And she went?'

'She went. And now she's in isolation in Bournemouth for her scruples,' added Mrs Shafto opening her eyes wide with amusement, 'waiting to see if she has what you've got. She's the two thousand five hundred and second contact.'

'What about you?'

'What do you think? The two thousand five hundredth and third!' This time she laughed and her black eyes looked piratical. 'Everyone in Beaudesert's a contact!' It was an angry laugh, but a laugh.

'She left a letter.'

'I won't read it now.'

A few moments passed. Outside, the fiery afternoon sun beat through the limp leaves of the chestnut tree shading the open window, and you could hear the insectile stir of traffic.

'I take it you're progressing all right? Tell me.'

'I feel better, I think, but it's a slow business. They gave me a psychiatrist for a bit because I suddenly found that I couldn't swallow.'

'Guilt!'

'What else?'

'Look what you've done!' Mrs Shafto suddenly began to sing which gave me a fright. 'What did you want to go and make those eyes for! Diddly, diddly, dee-dah! Look what you've done!'

I think she did it to make me laugh. But it didn't, for although her voice rather reminded me of Hutch, it sounded bitter.

'Oh dear, what a mess!' She closed her eyes and squeezed her face from brows to chin in a tired gesture. 'Oh what a mess.'

'Is it really all my fault?'

'I suppose I ought to say no!'

'But you *feel* it is?' I persisted.

'Not altogether. You've simply been the agent of disruption, haven't you? Like microbic Lenin locked up in his sealed carriage.'

'Or this bug bugging away in my gut?'

'I've been told by very wise people that true serenity of mind resides in the acceptance of these ghastly interpenetrations of our existence,' she said tiredly. 'I wish I didn't mind so much about my grandchildren. What's going to happen to them? The parents must look after their own affairs, I suppose. But look at Hugh! Such a fool! And Belle! Belle's even stupider!'

'I loved Belle.'

'What is love to you, Madame? Madness? Illness? Death?' she demanded irritably.

'You're perfectly right. It appears I began falling in love the moment I began incubating *S. Typhi.*'

'There you are! Oh, what folly!'

'And how can you prevent folly? Have you never been in love?'

'I've loved, of course, but I never let it affect the whole of me. I suppose I was trained not to. You see I'm a great believer in keeping irreconcilables separate.'

'What irreconcilables?'

'Oh!' she cried getting up to go. 'Body and spirit, reality and appearance, ideas and objects. I prefer order. I detest the bouillon of existence, it's so confusing and messy and impractical.'

'You don't sound absolutely convinced,' I remarked.

'You don't think so?' She smiled rather grimly. 'Keep that little thing watered. Tell the nurse, will you? Water from the bottom.'

'You'll come again?'

'I might if you'd like me to.'

'You'll come and tell me about what's going on at Beaudesert?' I said, 'because I'd like to know about Beaudesert.'

NINE

'He is a man of such outstanding sincerity,' Rosa was telling Dr Chieseman, 'a man of great probity and courage. As you know yourself the Rococo stands for everything aristocratic, everything the mob detests; it is barely acceptable to people nowadays, who can only find fault with the injustice of the economic forces which sustained it. The immorality of its patrons like poor Madame de Pompadour and that delightful Louis Quinze . . .'

'Yes, yes, yes,' cried Dr Chieseman impatiently. 'Yes!'

'Mr Shafto is keeping the "flame" burning,' cried Rosa loyally, 'against everybody!'

'What's the point?' demanded a pale-faced young man with sweet though curiously stale grey eyes, 'if it no longer has, if indeed it ever did, relevance?'

Rosa and Dr Chieseman turned on him with the speed of provoked kraits.

'Why on earth are you here then?' demanded Rosa furiously.

'To study the Enemy,' replied the young man coolly. He'd passed through the Marxist phase and was now playing with the idea of radical theology or, failing that, perhaps a D.Phil. in something or other.

'I agree,' came the unwanted voice of Margaret Crosroyde, 'that ideal, I mean of the cultivated individual, educated entirely at the community's expense . . .'

'Ideal, capital!' said Dr Chieseman, 'the only hope!'

'I didn't mean that,' cried Mrs Crosroyde. 'I should have said at the expense of the community. I happen to think that it's a crying disgrace . . .'

The long water spread like a geometric strip of trembling sky, and on the shade perimeter of Beaudesert's great trees, the limes, the enormous Wellingtonias, the Tradescant planes, the short grass was burnt to snuff. They sat on deck-chairs below the great chained boughs of an immensely old ilex tree. They were in fact prisoners themselves, which went far to explain their mutual short-temperedness. The evening before, Miss Lepper, the expert on Caffieri bronzes, had developed nose-bleeding, temperature and spots, and the M.O.H. had decreed that for the time being none of the members of the Rococo Symposium should be allowed to return to their homes in case they carried the Beaudesert plague to other parts of the United Kingdom.

What a comedown, Hugh thought as he approached over the dead grass; what a travesty of a Fête Galante! Their ugly bodies, their ugly clothes! Sitting in hideous deck-chairs. He took a deck-chair himself and shuffled his notes.

'I think,' he began, 'that in order to understand the spirit, the *essential* spirit of the Rococo we must, with Madame du Châtelet, begin by saying that we have nothing else to do in this world but to seek pleasant sensations!'

The doomed Symposium laughed politely, Rosa, from loyalty, rather too loudly. 'You might say,' he went on, 'that the devotees of this style insisted upon their right to "Heaven now", and to this end they invoked an ideal landscape, an empyrean of the mind, a vision both sensual and delightful of Heaven, which although it was a lie, and for that reason much criticised even at the time by the uncomprehending, yet had its own pathos . . .' He thought suddenly as he spoke of Watteau. He felt as withdrawn and as sad as a Watteau clown himself, nursing perpetually, in what felt like a gravid bruised heart, the memory of his ghastly row with Belle. He could remember quite clearly the heady moments before conquest when, transfixed by rage and jealousy and grief, he had waited to tell her what for so long she had been too damn stupid to see.

The temptation to tear down a rotten edifice is scarcely to be resisted. There is satisfaction, there is a sense of virtue even, in pulling down and stamping upon the disgusting claptrap of trumped-up convention, half-truths, overt lies and self-deception, which go to make up an unsatisfactory relationship. Yet the empty space left in the air by the collapse of the despised building can inspire shocked awe.

'Let us hear what de Tocqueville has to say about the morals of the then aristocracy,' he continued to the Symposium. '"It was no ordinary sight" he tells us, "to see a numerous and powerful class of men, whose every outward action seemed constantly to be dictated by a natural elevation of thought and feeling, by delicacy and regularity of taste, and by urbanity of manners . . ."'

'Hugh, I've got to tell you something—Hero's in love with me!' she'd said. Although her beautiful eyes were puffed and blotted with tears shed for Hero going into hospital, he could see that she was pleased. Pleased and flattered. His Belle, who should have been his sole and total property, sat weeping with apparently self-congratulatory grief before the bedroom glass. Anger, bottled up since long before Spring, gushed scaldingly into his chest.

'"Those manners,"' continued Hugh to the Symposium, 'and mark this! "threw a pleasant illusory charm over human nature, and though the picture was often false it could not be viewed without a noble satisfaction . . ."'

'Hero,' he'd said flatly to Belle, 'is my mistress!'

He repented the moment he'd said it. After all for sixteen weeks poor Belle had been deceitfully nurtured and cozened by Hero and himself into thinking that she was the cherished apex of a sentimental *ménage à trois*.

'What did you say?' She seemed to be growing huge. Elephantine. Swelling with outrage.

'No. Don't bother. Nothing!'

Where, oh where, had Belle gone then?

'Rococo,' he continued, 'was the enskyment of women, the making of them—albeit tongue in cheek—goddesses . . .'

In Belle's place on the bed lay a threshing maenad, tearing its clothes and moaning whenever he tried to go near it. Red-faced, snot-covered, a tear-blubbered sack, retching and trembling with rage and grief.

Rococo was fun. Rococo was gay. Existed by shocking and surprising. Why one painting had even included among clouds—an elephant!

Belle's maenad mood had been followed by one of calm so Olympian, so adamantine, as to be even more terrifying. Coldly she had denied him her bed. Next day she had left.

She had left just one day before Miss Lepper had developed nose-bleeding and spots, thus effectively preventing him from following her. She had gone, leaving no address and taking Jessica.

'The Departure from the Island of Cythera.' He evoked from the Symposium that portrait of Love's Sensibility; that sweet and aching dream of sighs and mists; soft hands on tender arms, warm lips at shell-pink ears, gently parting silk among the concealing leaves, all Nature conspiring . . . a scene scaldingly tender as the first touch of Love . . . bowing grasses, bright water, the naked, the very wanton amoretti . . .

At night after Belle had gone he'd lain awake and alone in the empty wastes of what he had once jokingly called their 'letto matrimoniale', madly wanting love, cursing Hero, hating himself. He'd thought of Rosa . . .

'In the end,' concluded Hugh, 'this delicate other dimension, this happy alternative, this refuge of the sceptical mind, torn between external nature and the mind's art, between knowledge and power, fell before the rising natural forces which destroyed it, and, as a brilliant critic has said: "Where the rococo had implied a life of leisure, the neo-classic [which followed it] promised hard work, discipline, and sacrifices at which even human blood might excitingly flow . . ."'

For a moment there was silence, and then to his surprise there was a flutter of applause, fading, like clapped pigeon wings, into the hot air. Then it came again. He was not sure what had happened. Somewhere a garden bell rang. One or two people rose and came towards him, though he didn't take in what they said. The others slowly, as in a dream, paired off, the pale and annoying young man, Mrs Crosroyde . . . for some reason he found their slow passage from beneath the tree to the house oddly moving. They were walking, he thought, like people doomed.

'It was good, Hugh,' Rosa was saying. 'You probably didn't realise it, but it was very good. You even impressed the Doctor here. I had only been telling him just before what a true champion of the "flame" you are . . .'

Hugh walked over to the house with them feeling strangely at peace within himself. That day, contrary to anything that he'd done before, he had luncheon in the cafeteria. Was it really his seminar he wondered or was it the threat of infection, the enforced seclusion, which in so short a time had altered the tone of the Symposium? The misery, the terrible sense of loss which he had been carrying about inside him had now changed to a kind of serene melancholy which, far from being painful was agreeable, almost sensually so. Moreover, this feeling of his seemed to be being shared by the other members of the encloistered Symposium.

The weather was continuing extravagantly hot, so that a rather continental style of life prevailed. Seminars beneath the chained ilex in the mornings, siestas in the cool bedrooms of the great house from luncheon until six, followed by drinks in the ornamental gardens. To bolster up everyone's spirits Hugh had seen to it that extra supplies of liquor were taken in.

As the days passed it became noticeable that the *genius loci* or whatever it was had actually begun to affect the members of the Symposium. It began sartorially. Those who had brought the correct clothes now changed in the evenings. Those who had not, repaired one night with Rosa to the Beaudesert attics where they went through a number of trunks containing an entire collection of nineteenth-century costumes. Garments were looked out, pressed and goffered, brushed, mended, finally put on, and Hugh, watching the actors as they loitered and lounged in the hot nights by urns and obelisks, began to realise how greatly human beings in fact added to the Beaudesert scene. And he found himself feeling glad that those seats, those paths, those waters had become so true a refuge, a place where in face of disease and death, phantasy of the most agreeable kind could be acted out.

By the ninth day of their imprisonment, Rosa and Dr Chieseman were taking regular walks together in the maze; by the eleventh they had exchanged life histories; by the thirteenth they had, without pain, drifted apart and Rosa's attention had been captured by Mark, the prospective theological student. By the fifteenth day, when it was confirmed that the lady expert on Caffieri bronzes really had got Phage 34, Rosa and Mark had begun an affair, and Dr Chieseman and Mrs Crosroyde were playing croquet without so much as a mention of Louis Quinze. By the seventeenth day, just before the hospital sent word that it wasn't Phage 34 after all but something very like it picked up on the Costa del Sol, everyone was spending the evenings discussing whether or not there was a God, or if not a God, whether there was some sort of intelligent 'intention' in the world. Hugh personally had discovered that Dr Chieseman's character was not so much arrogant as lacking in confidence. For when Hugh gave way to him on the superiority of the Swabian over the Bavarian style, he suddenly became quite tractable and charming. Even maddening Margaret Crosroyde dropped her frenetic radicalism and stopped calling plants by impossible names when Hugh, after too much whisky one evening, burst into tears by the great Urn of Friendship and confided his sad story, only just restraining himself from asking her to go to bed with him.

To be truthful, he had really looked for comfort in this quarter from Rosa. Never had Rosa's quick sympathy, passionate enthusiasm, large breasts seemed so desirable, but alas! it seemed that Rosa was already extending that very comfort of which he was in such need to the bad-mannered theological student. At this discovery he was concerned enough to crush down disappointment and lecture her gently for her own good.

'Hugh, what is happening to us all? It's being one of the strangest summers of my life. Do you know that in this fortnight I feel I've completely changed?'

'How changed?' he asked sternly.

'I think I have lost some of my prejudices, Hugh.'

'Nonsense, you have merely exchanged one prejudice for another.' Yet why, when you really came to think of it should one expect consistency of oneself let alone any other human being?

'No, Hugh, talking to Mark I feel, I *know* that I've been leading an inward-turning, unmeaningful, selfish, oh so selfish existence.'

'Oh Rosa! Rosa!' He began to laugh, then checked himself. 'Listen to me, Rosa, you haven't been persuaded here,' touching his head, 'only here!' vaguely indicating some point below his navel.

Her eyes became bright as licked stones and then with a warning catch of breath, 'Possibly,' she said with a dignity which impressed him, and then she added unfairly, 'I was once fond of you like that, Hugh, only you never even noticed!'

'Oh Rosa, what a beast I was!'

He bent down and kissed her gently, enjoying wistfully his loss. Yet he also felt happy for her. Glad, for he was genuinely fond of her, that she was escaping some trap that he himself might have to remain in for ever owing to his inability to adapt. He regretted, however, that her means of escape had to be the theological student; he seemed so exceedingly self-absorbed. Happily, however, Rosa had quite enough energy to absorb another's self absorption.

'And Hugh?' asked Rosa, her beautiful eyes spilling with sympathy, 'what, oh what is poor Hugh going to do now?'

'Ah,' said Hugh, 'I think that must depend upon Belle.'

Belle's letter lay in my hand. I balanced it there for some time after the door had closed on Mrs Shafto, guessing its contents, unwilling, oh most unwilling, even to open it.

'Hero.' The envelope carried that fine name that I had sullied. It was a round clear schoolgirl's hand, like a head monitor's, I thought. Nothing more. What had come over me? Yet as I opened it a painful retrospective flush of longing came again. Was it over then, or wasn't it?

'Hero, darling Hero. I don't really know what to think yet. As you probably know by now Hugh told me the whole thing. I still can't believe it, and it makes me feel such a fool that I was so self-obsessed and blind that I didn't see it at the time. It must have been so obvious. I can remember though how very happy it was before I did know, and that makes it possible for me to write to you.

'I really don't know what to say except that *practically* speaking (I wonder if you remember my saying that you can always, always do something?), practically speaking then, it might be helpful to you if I say that I'm sure you were ill for quite a long time incubating that wretched thing, *so not yourself.* As for me I was just outrageously flattered and conceited that you felt about me as you did. It's really dreadfully bad for one's ego, don't you think, to be loved? Well, that's what I think about the you and me part. As for the you and Hugh bit, the only practical thing I can say about that is that when it all began between you didn't know me, and if you *had* perhaps you *wouldn't* have, or would you?

'Oh dear! It's awful how these personal matters now seem so infinitely difficult and mysterious, so *out of hand*, if you know what I mean. They do honestly seem to put all the great issues like world poverty and the bomb etc. in the shade for a moment, don't they? And that's really humiliating. No wonder the big things can't go right if the small ones are in such a mess. I really believe, *practically speaking* (!) again, that it would be so much easier being President than living with another human being like you or Hugh (though living with you would have been easier!).

'I'm not sure what I'm going to do next. As Hugh's mother may have told you, I've jumped out of the frying pan into the fire and have been shut up in a frightful place here with nothing to do while I wait and see if I've got what you've got! I'm reading Peacock—not my kind of book really, but one of the only reasonable books here, and it's funny and true when you get into the swing of it. The characters remind me a bit of all of us! As you can imagine I feel terribly sick about it all sometimes, and more angry than I like being with Hugh—and you, but I do have remissions from this when I think about the truly happy times we had, and how the only thing that can be said is that at least we were and are all in it together.

'I'm writing to you in a remission, and getting it posted quickly before I get angry again. Don't try to answer it, I've made it impossible for you just in case!'

There was no address.

I lay there trying to recall the details of her face, but they were in shadow. I could only remember the rather annoying voice, and even that was fading. But how right she was! Life was an inexorable illness, though with remissions. One could comfort oneself or even inspire oneself with theories about it, but the actuality always, always, caught one off guard, as poor Belle and I had found out.

It had been a mild and gentle letter in full and admirable accordance with her beliefs, yet I didn't mention it when Katharine Shafto came again, because I didn't want to agitate further what were already clouded waters.

I was walking about the room when she came in. 'It's abating!' she announced. 'Only eight confirmed cases. It's now well and truly under control,' and then she read out a funny though sad story of how an unfortunate man-suspect had absconded from the hospital in his underpants and had had to be returned by the police on a magistrate's order.

'It's turning out to be a most unsatisfactory summer' (sitting by the open window and looking out). 'Hot, hot, hot, grass and trees like tinder, and my roses shattering in a morning! It's not at all how I'd have ordered it.'

'Would you like to have been God?' I asked idly.

'Yes!'

'And would you have been a jealous God?'

'Of my creation? Oh, very!'

I liked her. Not only because she had been the sole person apart from Dr Rabbinovitz who'd visited me, but because I enjoyed her disengagement from convention, her robustness. Her shortcomings amused me.

She came most days, plump, hoarse-voiced, imperious, leaving behind the pledges of her visits: choice miniature rock plants packed in moss; striped roses and lilies sprinkled carefully with water to keep them fresh; globular saffron gooseberries on a leaf. She transformed my desolate desert room with creatures from the outer world, her world, earnests of her return.

Why did she come? I don't know. Perhaps I amused her, though in conversation she tended to be opinionative and often rather destructive. Yet I enjoyed it, quarrelling with her about books and painting and personalities and politics, though I never dared touch upon those deeper matters to which I resorted as soon as she closed the door; those matters which had once concerned Hugh and Belle, and me, and which now rendered down into the timid question as to what I was going to do with my own life.

A week before I was due to leave the hospital she came again, and as she nipped away dead heads and weeds and faded leaves, she asked me, 'Well, what about your convalescence?'

'I haven't thought yet.'

'Come back and stay with me.'

Yet she came neither the next day nor the next, and it was only on the day that I actually went out myself that they told me she was under observation as a Phage 34 suspect herself.

TEN

I was to go to Marly, Julia shrieked when I telephoned her for details about Mrs Shafto's illness. The Signora had insisted on this before the ambulance had taken her away. If I wanted to visit her I could visit her as easily from Marly as anywhere.

The taxi that fetched me from the hospital was hot as an oven, and even when I rolled down the window the air that came in seemed already exhausted. In the Beaudesert streets the awnings dangled limply, and in the heat the chestnut leaves were shrivelled before their time. There were hardly any people about.

'This bloody epidemic's just about finished everyone,' the taxi driver said. 'Filthy thing! All come from people not washing their hands properly after going to the toilet!'

Beaudesert's pretty over-preserved houses and shop fronts quivered in the petroleum-charged heat; façades, I knew; indeed, only I knew what they concealed. The unendurable self-disgust of those first days in hospital had returned full force. My mind was clogged with images of blocked pipes, of sewage pressed down and running over, seeping through cracks, percolating through soft pink bathroom paper on to fingers never afterwards washed before they were plunged into the steaming bowls of meat to grapple out gobbets. I felt run-down and still sick. Katharine Shafto being a suspect meant of course only one thing, that I, in those hectic days of convalescence after the car crash, had somehow infected her.

'Through the park?' the man asked, and I said 'Yes.' It was possible and actually easier to get to Kate Shafto's by way of Beaudesert's southern entrance.

Yet even here there was no cool. The sky seemed void of air, and, bulking its hideous shape within it, was the winking scaly pile of Beaudesert. Down the straight, urn-marked rides could be seen the hot expanses of the ginger gravel parterres, and running along beside them, reflecting the colourless sky, were metallic sheets of glittering water. The level had gone down in the heat, leaving slimy green rinds at the pools' edges. It was only when the taxi rumbled over the cattle grid which spanned the ha-ha dividing Beaudesert from the old gravel-workings that I heard the first bird, a ring-dove, billing from the shade of one of Kate Shafto's thickets. It was a watery sound as though somewhere in all this fiery heat there might, after all, be a cool spring gurgling. Then the lane twisted, and through the trees I could see water moving, and then all at once the old house presented itself, humorously almost, as though at the last moment it had leapt out in welcome from the shading trees where it had long been concealed in anticipation waiting.

I endured, because I had to, Julia's and the pug's ululations in full sunlight.

'The Signora?'

'Tanta malata . . . very eel,' cried Julia. 'Peccato! ma credo non typhoid!'

'What makes you think that?'

'Credo!'

'Have you heard from the hospital?'

'No, the Signorina Kinoull will see when she goes this evening.'

I took the large cup of tea Julia made me down to the edge of the water and knelt in the grass under the willow, and saw through its branches the small islands, vaporised by heat, jumping about like green flames in an azure sea. 'As is the garden so is the gardener,' they say, the Chinese I think. So what did this garden reveal of Mrs Shafto whom I hardly knew?

It was less a garden perhaps than a miniature natural region, like Bacon's garden at Gorhambury which Aubrey had seen though too late, for by that time it had been ploughed up and its clear waters were overgrown with flags and rushes. Her material, if I were to believe Hugh, had originally been a chaos of puddle and churned subsoil left from the old gravel-workings. What, I wondered, had been the first stage in the sequence? Had the design been waiting ready formed in her imagination, or had the whole affair been so conceived that, given its first momentum, the rest had followed of its own accord? What had been the first step? Perhaps she had imported topsoil, planted trees, and the rest had then followed naturally, for her hand seemed to have touched it very lightly, merely guiding the matter at her disposal into banks and glades and water-runnels from which afterwards had come the fish and birds and worms and butterflies . . . there it was, a small kingdom so ordered that it ran on its own, equipped with its own poise and counter-poise. I was of course too ignorant then to have known anything about ecology, about the technique of groundcover for instance, or the careful matching of predator with quarry. I could only see the completed creation, which of course was never complete, but restless like its macrocosm, changing constantly.

But she worked not only with living material. There was that other interest, an odd one for a woman of her age and period, those model sailing-ships dry-docked in the reed-thatched boathouse where the swans nested, each plank and gunwale shaped by her neat powerful fingers during the winter nights she spent in her workroom.

What does a love for the miniature suggest? As a race the English seem peculiarly fascinated by it. Their literature abounds in instances; there were Bacon's miniature islands, there were my uncle Toby's model fortifications on the bowling-green, and Commander Trunnion's model quarter-deck complete with cannon; there was the fort and drawbridge of Mr Wemmick's Ancient. Perhaps the English simply enjoy a certainty of power, however restricted. Perhaps they just like playing at being God.

'Flowers from Arcadia!' I said when I went in to see her early that evening. 'I hope to Heaven I haven't picked anything that I shouldn't?'

She looked tired and restless, raised herself on an elbow to make sure that I really hadn't picked anything that mattered, and then subsided back on to her pillows without a word.

'No news yet of your tests?'

'They say later on tonight.'

'I'm so sorry this has happened.' She didn't answer. 'Say something,' I said. 'You know quite well that if you've got it, it's I who've given it to you. Try and think how I'm feeling.'

'Oh, this disgusting interpenetration of thoughts, bodies, germs,' she mused unkindly, 'making us willy-nilly all one, confounding everything that God in his great wisdom was at such pains to make individual and separate!'

'That's unlike you!'

She smiled slightly. She lay, a pole-axed general, an imprisoned admiral, a disgraced colonial governor, staring moodily over the hospital sheets with gloomy cinnamon-coloured eyes.

'Do say something—please.'

'Say what? That you can console yourself that if I have got it there are worse people than you to get it from? Will that do? Is that what you want?'

She propped herself up in bed, examined the honey-suckle that I had brought her with a stern expression, pinched out the greenfly that I could now see were infesting it, and fell back on the pillows, her eyes dark arrow slits:

'Actually, it was probably a camembert I ate. Julia says so and she usually knows.'

At that I began to laugh, out of relief I think. She was already laughing, and we laughed until a nurse, like an irritable pullet, put her head round the door and said I'd have to go if I went on disturbing Mrs S. like that.

'As is the garden so is the gardener.' I couldn't get this out of my head. When I got back the sun had gone down and the air was cool, and cooler still on the water when I took out Katharine Shafto's rowing boat. I did this with some sense of trespass as though, staring over the gunwale at the reflection of the white moon tossing and brightening in its watery basket of weed, listening to the owls calling from her trees and watching them flap slowly over the narrow moonlit channels that separated her islands, I was somehow seeing into the recesses of her spirit. So I charted her, sailing over the reflected calm of the night sky, circling her islands. When I landed on one of them, moving so smoothly from water to the beach of grating pebbles, I felt the grass and it was tinder dry, and the ash-leaves which had looked so green from the house crackled in my hands, their twigs brittle as baked fishbones, and the bark of the trees was warm too, almost as if the trees were feverish.

When I got back the drawing-room was in darkness, its curtains unpulled, its windows open on to the water which was now as still as glass, though thin, flocky webs of reflected moonlight flew about the room. It was odd being there without her, gazing at what she'd made.

Nowadays, I reflected, people don't die very readily of typhoid. A two-per-cent mortality. But just suppose she did die? Then, unsustained, this whole small world would disintegrate. I now piled tragedy upon tragedy as it is my histrionic nature to do, seeing her planted trees throttled with ivy, crashing into the waters where they collected morsels of surface wrack, sprang aquatic thorns and carr, while across the neglected fields I could see winding a new cinder track along which the Beaudesert Council dust-carts rumbled on afternoons hot as this one had been, to tip their mountains of sweet glittering refuse so loved by gulls, filling up with bottles and tins and plastic the coastal waters of her archipelago, while her house, forsaken (for who would buy it?), fell in, ran back into the ground again, became a desert of nettles, which were sprayed, bulldozed and concreted over to make the car park the Council needed so badly.

Then the phone brayed. It brayed triumphantly again and again, but before I could get to it Julia was there.

Julia was right. It had been the camembert. The symptoms had been most suggestive, but the blood and serum test had disclaimed *S. Typhi*. The Signora Shafto would be home in the morning.

'I was fortunate because my father understood me very well,' said Mrs Shafto complacently. She looked paler and rather thinner but otherwise fit. 'It was only when I left home and went out into the world as you might say that I discovered what an absurd place it actually was. My father had a workshop like I have here, and in there we invented steamers—dear little twin-cylinder marine engines—we used to try them out in the experimental hulls we built on the lake.'

'You had a lake?'

'Yes, always a lake,' said Mrs Shafto. 'Children must have water to be happy; you can't do anything without water; it's the beginning of everything after all, isn't it? Everything in the first instance comes from water, doesn't it?'

'But the absurdity of the world?' I pressed. We sat in the world, or at least we sat in Mrs Shafto's version of it. Mrs Shafto was wearing her large Greek peasant's straw hat and indeterminate gardening clothes covered by a striped fishmonger's apron. We were having tea.

'Well, I found it difficult to reconcile the life within with the reality without. You see, strange as it may seem, I quite often felt so wise and brave inside though I was treated, being a girl, like a sort of idiot, though mercifully not by my father. It was criminal, looking back, and I was quite right not to accept it. I was a brown, strong, bullying little girl.' Katharine Shafto began to laugh and then, like a dove cooing, to wheeze.

'In shooting butts, I do remember them quite well, unfortunate women! Bitten to death, covered with pearls, sometimes diamonds. Bitten,' she added, 'not of course by the dogs—by mosquitoes. I didn't want to be one of those. I'd rather have done the shooting myself. Nor did I want to be one of those women who are eternally matching. You know, the mauve of the hat with the mauve of the gloves . . . oh dear!'

'What did you do then?'

'I think it's cosmic,' said Mrs Shafto, paying no attention, 'the absurdity, though less perhaps in simple countries. People have since called it the Absurd, and they're quite right. It's about the one thing Hugh and I are agreed upon. He says fathers have daughters, mothers have sons, and that's quite absurd enough to begin with. This means that men can get shut up in women's bodies and women in men's bodies; just as slaves are shut up in kings' bodies, kings in slaves', black in white, white in black. You can develop the theme ad infinitum and even then you haven't really dealt with the body itself, which beats everything for sheer preposterousness, doesn't it? Then there's the extraordinary nature of the world outside it. I mean, here we are!' cried Mrs Shafto laughing.

'Driven by the pesterings of nature to live until we meet the oncoming surety that we shall die. What's your answer to it?'

'What's yours?' countered Mrs Shafto, turning her large hat towards me. 'I don't really feel like discussing myself at present.'

'I take refuge in the past,' I said, 'and I've been most sharply criticised for it by too many of my friends, who thought it not only defeatist but selfish and unhealthy.'

'How wrong they were,' murmured the hat. 'A love for the past indicates a desire for heaven.'

'That's called phantasy.'

'Phantasy,' said Mrs Shafto, 'is nothing to be ashamed of.'

'I didn't realise that you were a Christian.'

'I'm not, but unlike you perhaps I don't confuse heaven with an afterlife. The one I'm sure of, the other I find rather problematical.'

'They dislike phantasy nowadays because, they say, it's untruthful.'

'On the contrary, it's a very important aspect of truth,' said Mrs Shafto. 'When will people see that truth doesn't exhaust reality, and that in the unreduced remainder may be truths belonging to our peace? No!' wagged the hat, 'I'd say that your love of the past is a perfectly normal desire to recall heaven. Once we acknowledge that, then a love of the past will also be seen as a love of the future, so that only leaves the present.'

'You go too quickly, and as for the present, that's the really difficult tense.'

'Everyone, all trying to reproduce their memoir of heaven in their own way,' pondered Mrs Shafto, taking no notice.

'They produce hell.'

'Exactly the same principle only in reverse,' said Mrs Shafto shortly. 'Tell me,' and she creaked round in her basket chair like a restless dog, 'why did you commit adultery with my son?'

'I never thought of it as adultery, I must say. Perhaps it was something to do with the past, both of us being so besotted with it. It's a great bond, you know, one of the strongest.'

'Not love?' asked Mrs Shafto. 'I hoped for his sake, though I doubted him capable of it, that it might have been love.'

'Well, yes, love too, though I think I'm rather shapeless about love, easily influenced. I've had lovers before.'

'Lovers? Shapeless?'

'I feel a curiously indeterminate person. I feel like the future participle in Latin. *Futurus*, is it? Anyway, about to be made. I had no parents, they were killed in Borneo and I was brought up by a fool of an aunt who was a freethinker and so she sent me to a progressive school.'

'Progressive school?'

'Where we did what we liked, so I've always done what I liked.'

'So I should imagine.'

'To love "meaningfully", as they'd say nowadays,' (the hat stirred) 'it seems one needs obstacles.'

'Tell me about Belle.'

'Well, Belle was hardly an obstacle. In the end it all turned into rather an obscene *ménage à trois,* though perhaps it wasn't really obscene, and actually a kind of Tahiti situation instead, and therefore immensely desirable. I can't make up my mind about it.'

'Don't you think Belle is really rather a stupid woman?' asked Mrs Shafto. 'So terribly mechanistic in her outlook?'

'Belle is one of the few people who makes an honest effort to turn phantasy into reality,' I said sternly.

'Nevertheless, she fails,' jeered the hat, 'fails because she's stupid. And in point of fact, she isn't honest, as you claim; she deludes herself. In fact she hasn't even approached honesty.'

'Nearer perhaps than Hugh or me,' I said. 'I'm in a state of continual retreat hardly to be concealed, and Hugh cheats himself by pretending that he's guarding the flame of civilisation. I wouldn't mind so much if his version of the flame weren't the Rococo, which is really the corruptest, the most enervating, the most specious . . .'

'. . . and the funniest!' said the hat unexpectedly. 'Remember, also the funniest. You mustn't persist in only seeing in part like that!'

And so we went on wrangling agreeably until the sun went down and she disappeared to damp down her greenhouse.

'I must speak to you. I want to speak to you!'

I didn't want to see Hugh. I simply wanted to idle my time away in Kate Shafto's garden doing nothing and waiting for something to happen of its own accord, just as

I'd done when I'd been trapped between Hugh and Belle. I felt sure that in the end something would happen, and I wasn't really worried.

'I've got to get things straight,' Hugh said over the telephone. 'I'm simply not going to go on like this!'

'Like what?'

'Not knowing where I am.'

'Who does?' I asked.

'Well, at least that makes two of us, and that's a bit more matey, you must admit.'

'But I love it! Not knowing!'

He walked down to Marly by the long water. But this evening the carefully raked gravel, the large urns festooned with pan-pipes, goats' feet, grapes, wreathed in stone vine-leaves and ribbons, depressed him. It was hot, hotter now than it had ever been in the past jading three weeks. He saw that the place looked empty, like a deserted ballroom. Given a clean bill of health, the members of the Symposium had gone home. He missed them. He missed them loafing about in the grateful shade of the arboretum; he missed them dallying in the green rides or moping by the ornamental waters. He realised again with the same shock, for it was still an unfamiliar notion to him, that if only for aesthetic reasons gardens like Beaudesert's had been expressly designed to be populated; had been designed, literally, as fun and pleasure grounds. With the warm dust of the parterres stirring beneath his feet, he mentally moved on to the odd reflection that it was not only aesthetically that the presence of the once-dreaded people had pleased him, but companionably, too. This explained an otherwise bewildering discontent with the urns. He had to face it, as he stopped for a moment to destroy the too perfect reflection of a gazebo with a petulant handful of grit, that he missed, quite separately and uniquely, dreadful Dr Chieseman, calamitous Margaret Crosroyde, and, with a great deal of his mind and body, dear Rosa.

It was all due, of course, to the horror of Belle leaving. That had created an appalling vacuum. When something like that happened you had to cling on for dear life to everyone and anyone, even to Margaret Crosroyde. And you strained your guts to please and communicate, everlastingly grateful for every crumb of sympathy.

It was owing to Belle's precipitate action that Beaudesert had tragically, and in accordance with its beautiful and evil name, truly become for him a desert where owls hooted and bears drank. And yet, for important shifts of attitude take place unnoticed often in the shadow of great events, Belle's absence in its own way had been a release. He had greatly enjoyed their enjoyment of his seminars, and after self-analysis he realised with some surprise that his former attitudes must, up to a point, have been synthetic, assumed to please, or, more likely, to annoy Belle. It had been a normal response to the peculiar nature of their sexual relationship, as well as an answer to her particular and patient philistinism.

Annexed to these small but important self-discoveries was another, perhaps not such an occasion for self-congratulation. This was the realisation that now everything was at an end, he was being smoothly and inexorably drawn back to Marly, to his mother and to Hero. He knew that about Hero he felt curiously ambivalent, uncertain whether he was going to be wildly angry or madly in love with her.

He reached the end of the long water. The sight of its intermittent urns, its clipped yew, stirred some old thought in his mind, recalled from long-ago lines, verse of some kind. He strode over the rough grass on the perimeter towards the ha-ha and the ride through his mother's plantations. It was sad that he hadn't brought Margaret Crosroyde to see Marly, or even Dr Chieseman. He grieved over this lost opportunity; they would have enjoyed it. In the intimacy generated by their true study of the Rococo, they had all moved, since every style contains the thrilling seeds of its own destruction, from what was in a high degree artificial to what was unquestionably simple. They would have enjoyed Marly, and he would have enjoyed showing it to them.

Gnats rained ceaselessly through the hot gold air; below his feet heavy blackbirds scattered complainingly into the rustling leaves:

> How vainly men themselves amaze
> To win the Palm, the Oak or Bayes;
> And their incessant Labours see
> Crown'd from some simple Herb or Tree.

He must have learned this at school, but couldn't remember what came next or even who'd written it.

Then through the leaves his mother's place came in sight, and he glimpsed her irregular waters and saw, as the sky closed to dusk, a moon rising, and at that moment the missing lines came effortlessly to him:

While flowers and all Trees do close
To weave the Garlands of repose!

This was true of his mother's place. The seeming effort-
lessness of her art contrasted with what was so contrived
and obvious at Beaudesert.

He could now see in the fading light someone who
must surely be Hero sitting on a garden chair beside the
willow which grew by the thatched boathouse.

'Hello, Hero!'

'Hello!'

'Hugh?' called his mother, coming out of the house
with some glasses on a tray.

'It's over then,' Hero said, 'over and finished with, your
Symposium?'

'Yes.'

'Was it so very bad after all?'

There was a short silence, and she was sorry she'd said
it, the thoughtless words of sympathy which recalled too
much perhaps of what had gone before the Symposium:
all the love and sex and danger and illness and desertion.

'I wonder if you can believe it, but I've been flattered
into submission,' said Hugh laughing. 'I like people!
It's always what's unexpected that carries the citadel,
isn't it?'

She thought, 'Good God, he must have *known* that
conceit was his weak point,' but remarked at the same time
that the slackening of tension she had perceived in him,
the shift of being that she'd intuited as he'd come over
the grass had not been imagined. Hugh for his part was
feeling immensely relieved that he was, after all, going to

be neither wildly angry nor yet madly in love, but a sort of interesting combination of both.

'I'm afraid you're too fond of showing off,' said his mother. 'The odd thing is that tyrants are always moved by the crowd; that's why there are tyrants.'

'Oh, I was never a tyrant!' said Hugh, still smiling.

They drank something vaguely nautical that Kate Shafto had concocted. It was plainly exceedingly powerful.

'I must say you adapt extraordinarily well,' Hugh said the moment his mother's back was turned.

'Don't you adapt too? You look so well that you must have been adapting.'

'I mean first me, then Belle, and now mother, all of us quite, quite different!'

'I always told you I was shapeless, shapeless and rather over-anxious. Hugh dear, it is safely over between us isn't it?'

'Yes. No. In one way perhaps.' He felt an annoying resurgence of tenderness at the very thought that it might be all over.

'I'm so sorry about everything, but I expect Belle'll come back to you.'

'What about you and Belle, then? That's really what I wanted to talk to you about.'

'I hardly know. Perhaps I feel about Belle like you do about me. It was so extremely painful at the time. I felt so desperate. I've wondered since if it was a kind of symptom of the typhoid. After all, it coincided exactly with my gestating it, or whatever the correct word is.'

'I think you mean incubating.'

'What about you? What are you going to do?'

'No, I want to hear about your plans, you're the crucial, the dangerous one, if you don't mind my saying.'

'Hugh, if you like I'll go away when Belle comes back.'

'Well . . . no, let's wait and see, it may not be necessary.'

The heat closed about them. Above Mrs Shafto's waters the constellations glittered.

'Belle wrote me such a kind letter when I was in hospital.'

'I'm glad, very glad.'

'I feel such peace now. Do you think we'll be at one another's throats tomorrow?'

'No,' Hugh said, 'no.'

Mrs Shafto returned with a fresh mix of whatever it was and a candle.

'Look at the flame,' Hero said, 'it's hardly moving.'

'Do you know that on the clipper *Thermopylae*,' said Katharine Shafto inconsequentially as she refilled their glasses, 'a man could hold a candle with an unshaded flame with the ship doing seven knots?'

'What does that tell us?'

'Practically speaking, that the ship was incredibly sensitive to the lightest play of the breeze; metaphysically it says something beautiful that I can't understand.'

'I think it's a kind of parable.'

'You're perfectly right, a kind of parable.'

The drink was exceedingly strong.

'What's in it?' Hero asked after a time-lapse in which no one had made any attempt at conversation. 'Oh, your mother isn't here!'

'Some amazing mixture,' Hugh said. 'My grandfather spent one part of his life in the Japanese navy.'

'Do you think it's *saki*?' For some reason they began to giggle. Mrs Shafto was nowhere to be seen.

'Perhaps it's strega. Strega means a witch. Isn't your mother rather a witch?'

'Yes.'

'You know, we're tighter than we thought.'

'But I feel quite clear, don't you?'

'Yes, perfectly clear.'

'Not nauseous?'

'Not nauseous in the least.'

He laid his hand gently on Hero's arm. She turned and he kissed her softly on the mouth.

'That's nice. That's happy. All's well?'

'Yes, except where is she?'

They peered into the darkness above the fleecy gold nimbus of the candle-flame.

'There's something,' Hugh said, 'but I can't quite see it. Do you mind if I blow out the candle?'

The moon had risen, was irradiating with peppery silver the hot night air. Then they saw it. A swan, or was it a ship? It was hard to tell at that distance, for though the water broke to silver at its breast it was so dark that you could distinguish no hull.

It was set full sail towards the archipelago, and, as they stood up to track it, it vanished for a moment behind one of the smaller islands, then re-emerged, white and burning with reflected moonlight.

'Let's swim and catch her!'

Only drink could have made it possible for their clothes to fall so effortlessly from them, could have caused that sweet amorousness with which, hand in hand as at Cythera, they walked naked into the soft black water.

It was effortless swimming, too. The ship, for now they could see that it was a ship, was moving smoothly, its translucent sail tautened by an unfelt breeze. It slipped soundlessly past the islands like a moon through clouds.

'Turn back!' shouted Hugh suddenly. 'It's too cold!' And then she felt below them, at what depth she couldn't gauge, something that felt like an enveloping net of freezing weed, though it was without actual substance.

'It's a cold spring!' shouted Hugh. 'Turn back!'

But it was not to be evaded, seemed almost to follow them, netting them, impeding them, however hard they struggled against its freezing web.

The black cold moved to the thighs, to the stomach, to the lungs, to the heart. A torso only, she rocked forward, the night water blinding her to the moon and the bird or the ship. She tried to kick out, but the black ubiquitous web clung round her mouth, was breathed in and expelled gushing from her nostrils. She felt from a distance that she was pushing against a substance that was yielding and cold as brawn. Death. It tightened around her, and she struggled again and again, beginning to lose consciousness. There was an arrest. Then far beneath her she felt her flesh dragging over sharp points of gravel, and then the moon or the bird began to swell painfully in her drowned eyes, spilling out from under her lids hot and painful as tears. Above her she could hear a voice repeating the same thing over and over again, and the flabby brawn which she had pushed against so fiercely, and which in fact was Hugh, was complicated suddenly by the addition of a dry hand. It was a hard, cool, rough hand, and her smoky voice pierced Hero's marine ears.

'Oh, you little fool. Whatever were you trying to do?'

She tried to explain about the swan or the ship or the moon or whatever it had been, but was unable to, and instead vomited rum-tainted water over the stones, then fell to hiccuping and retching, a stranded white cod in the moonlight.

'Too strong drink I'm afraid,' said Mrs Shafto, 'Oh, much too strong. Very, very wrong of me. I only thank God you're alive!'

'It was beautiful,' Hugh told her later. 'You must have known perfectly well how beautiful it was,' he said accusingly to his mother.

'I truly didn't think of it being dangerous,' she said. 'It's something I do quite often on my own you know, sailing the boats at night, though I must admit I haven't done it with people here before.'

She laid her hand over her son's for an instant. He was shocked to feel how rough it was, more like a workman's hand.

'I know it was dangerous, but I can't help being rather proud that you saw it,' she said.

ELEVEN

In all the excitement of what had so nearly been a drowning tragedy, Katharine Shafto forgot her ship. It lay, beached in shingle on the far shore of the gravel pit, its sails fluttering gently in the freshening wind. It lay, like some dreaming swan, one hour, two hours perhaps, while the lights from the house went out, until only one, probably Kate Shafto's continued to burn over the water.

Tight, cocky, curly, pent-up, spoiling and jolly for anything, five of them found it on their way back from the town in the early hours of the morning. Seeing water through the trees they'd paddled their throbbing machines through the long hay of the field, wanting to swim.

They pushed the boat a little way out into the lake, and for a while hurled half-bricks and stones at it, then one with more imagination waded out, dragged it ashore, soaked a piece of rag in his petrol tank and squeezed the spirit over the sails and bulwarks. Then he turned the ship about and set her on course for the islands. Her splashed sails sucked and swelled and then, lame as she was, she began gathering way, so that if he hadn't moistened the match head with spittle to make a slow flame before striking it and hurling it after her, she might have got away untouched. As it was there was a rush of air, and a kind of suppressed explosion as the sails ignited, and, the wind quickening just at that moment, the ship drew away, morsels of flaring rag blowing from her shrouds.

Caught by her rather awesome beauty they were silent, watching her for a moment, then they cheered as, gathering speed, the fire-ship was carried flaming out of sight between two of the islands.

Now, because they no longer had her, the ship, like a bird or a fish or a woman that had got away, became an object of passionate desire.

'Come on!'

'Come on!'

The three of them who could swim were unzipping their boots, peeling away the heavy black husks of clothing from their lean white bodies, casting aside the grotesque insectile crash helmets. In a moment they were thrashing about in the disturbed black water.

Her sails half-consumed, the ship was already losing way, would soon be within reach, though fragments of burning sail were still blowing from the rigging. As she passed unscathed through a narrow channel between two islands, one of these fragments hovered, still burning in the air, and then it dropped, nestling in the dry grass like a bird seeking shelter. From this point it wasn't long before flame began to ripple outwards. A ring of fiery ferns which sprang swiftly to bracken, then, sapling height, spreading all the time. The ship, flames playing like St Elmo's fire about her spars, drifted into the centre of the lake.

It was at this moment that I saw it. I'd pulled back the curtains, thinking that it was the morning sun playing through them. Instead I saw an armillary of burning hair, an illuminated glass ship.

With the acid light of the moon in my eyes I'd been dreaming all night of drowning. I'd woken to sink back into sleep again, dreaming this time that I was dancing some kind of grotesque highland fling with Hugh and his mother. It had turned into a dance as involved as one in a Khajuraho temple relief, with Hugh caressing my loins, which in the dream had felt cold and heavy as suet beneath his touch, while his mother caressed all of me above the navel which blazed and sang with heat, my ears and eyes and nostrils filled with a hilarity of gold bees.

As I watched the bulwarks of the ship went black, a weak flame guttered for a moment at its waterline and was soused. I had expected darkness to fall after that and only now I saw that the night was still alight, and that there was a roaring sound like waters rushing together, and the smell, delicious as food, of burning wood. So at last it came to me that the archipelago itself was on fire.

The wind, the first in weeks, had got up, and before it, flames like ripped banners were flaring through Mrs Shafto's copses, the trees seeming to flaunt their flaming leaves until they, like the ship, went out, crashing to the ground in showers of sparks.

I stood there, not moving, seeing that where the ship had been, objects like bodies seemed to be floating in the turbulent blood-coloured water, and above the cascade-like roaring of the flames I thought I could hear shouting. It was a scene Delacroix might have painted, terrible as his 'Raft of the *Meduse*', for now I could see that the floating objects were men thrashing and struggling in the water. I could see too that a boat had put out from the shore.

It advanced in jerky silhouette towards the wreck, looking oddly comical. I wanted to cheer, for through the smoke I could just make out that Hugh was rowing, with his mother in the stern. It was now obvious that what I'd taken to be bodies breaking the red water were men swimming—or trying to swim.

I broke away from the window then, went crashing down the staircase, half falling, and out into the night. Julia was standing like a fisherman's widow on the shore, her hand shading her eyes from the glare.

First I shook her, that vast, noisy, fat woman, then, shouting, I demanded whether she'd rung for help. She shook off my arm and continued to stare at the rowing boat.

'If I were the Signora I'd kill them,' she said. 'I'd just let them drown.'

They'd stopped rowing. The small boat was rocking about in the angry red light, and three heads were converging on it, two rather closer than the third. I could see the rosy light from the flames catching their cheeks. For a moment it looked as though the boat would capsize as they clawed at its sides, and above the crackling of the fire I could hear Hugh shouting, and I could see his struggling outline as he and his mother swayed this way and that trying to pull the great spent youths to safety. I also noticed that the third head had disappeared.

The wind was abating, and a fine rain had begun to fall, and there was a weak yellow light marking the east.

This light grew steadily stronger until it dulled the light shed by the tattered flames. During this time they succeeded in bringing two shivering boys ashore, one clinging to the gunwale of the boat, the other half-naked, lying with chattering teeth in its bottom. Then as, too late, the fire engines came braying through the lightening lanes, through sleeping Beaudesert, through the park and over the cattle grid, Hugh and his mother were turning back for the missing boy. They rowed again and again round the spot where they'd last seen him until, in the drizzling half-light, the policemen who'd arrived hailed them in so that they could take over.

The police stayed doggedly on and on until at last, just after midday, their grappling hooks drew up the drowned boy. They laid him at the water's edge, swollen and plum-coloured, like a hog too long soaked in brine, of a piece with the dead landscape. For, as with him, the destruction of Marly was complete. The grouching away of the water meadows in the first instance could scarcely have presented a view of greater desolation than poor Marly did now. Gone her thickets and dells and copses, gone, for there had been one, the very genius of the place. The rain now drove unimpeded through the blackened branches of the trees and diluted to ink the carbonised earth of a monochrome landscape.

When they found the boy, Kate Shafto got out of bed where she'd been lying since early morning. Stocky and sad in her nautical macintosh, she raised the corner of the blanket with which they'd covered him and gazed silently at his sleeping drowned face.

'I don't know him,' she said.

'Finality,' she said later on. 'What I suppose Belle would call reality, something to which one has no choice but to submit. And it was my beautiful boat that caused it!'

She stared unblinkingly into the rain as she was speaking, and then began to walk slowly round the rim of what had once more become a gravel pit.

'You once told me how in love you were with the past,' she said stopping after we'd walked a little way. 'Well, what does all this say to you?'

I could hardly tell her how, all at the same time, it both horrified and excited me. Much as reading about the sack of Rome does, or the six-week-long burning of the library at Alexandria.

'Tout passe, tout casse, tout lasse,' I said knowing it was facile, and of course I spoke only of her islands. The boy's death was impossible to take in. Belle, I thought, might actually have been able to understand it, or at least have been able to explain it within some kind of logical structure as just one more example of the endless, endless deprivation of the already deprived. 'To him that hath not shall be taken away, even that little that he hath.'

'Tout passe is tout lazy!' said Mrs Shafto sharply. 'I want to know what has happened. Tell me, what has happened?'

She stood there, water running off her conquistador's nose, her eyes half-closed against the fine soaking rain.

'Nothing,' I said helplessly, 'especially the boy. Nothing, nothing, nothing. The boy as far as I know wasn't even interesting. Marly was. Nothing!'

'Not nothing,' she said, picking up this conversation hours later. 'Absence is different from nothing, surely? It isn't the same thing. Surely it's the absence that makes the past interesting. The fact that something was there once and isn't any longer?'

'I suppose so.'

'I think so,' and she stopped again. 'Where is the past?'

So because I thought that such abstractions might solace her I said, 'You tell me.'

'Do you think that the destruction may after all be unimportant?' she said. 'Of the garden I mean. Of course, I haven't the right or the courage to say a word about that boy or his poor mother. That is too terrible. I can't say anything about that. But with the garden, would the real destruction have been the eclipse of the dream, that garden of the heart's and mind's and soul's eye? That personal and private view of heaven which exists and of which this was after all only the poor copy? I mean, suppose we were like animals and could conceive of no other condition than the one we were in. Imagine there being no "other" to console us. Even in phantasy?'

'You're speaking of the enormous power, magic almost, that the vision gives you.' I suddenly thought then of how much Belle had admired that great last speech of Martin Luther King's. His vision of the New World.

'Provided I have the ideal in my mind, I really don't need to go gardening again,' said Mrs Shafto.

'Thy will be done in earth as it is in heaven!'

'Ah, well,' she said. 'I probably will then. It looks so ugly.'

'I'll help you.'

So I did. June deteriorated into a grey windy July which in its turn gave way to an exhausting humid August. By this time the grass had begun growing on the islands again, so that they looked like dusty black buns quilled with cheerful-looking angelica.

Our days became ordered, the sort of mechanical order which I have often noticed can be the precursor of regeneration. It was an order I enjoyed because it lengthened time so wonderfully. We started off at nine each morning piling saws, mattocks, slashers and God knows what into the small boat; then we rowed over to the blackened evil-smelling islands. We cleared them meticulously, one by one, of charred trees and brushwood and the calcined skeletons of birds and small animals that had been trapped by the holocaust. We made further great fires of this rubbish, day after day, until all that remained of leaves and thrushes and squirrels and lizards was consumed and scattered by our rakes into soft grey ash over the earth.

'For God's sake do take it easy or you'll have a seizure!' I said. Between moments of indolence when she'd stare absently over the chaos before her, perhaps recasting it in imagination, she'd work with a terrific gusto that I was sure was bad for her. Often I got nervous that I wasn't doing things right, because I frequently annoyed her by my lack of dexterity. Once when I was rocking a gaunt mast-like stump back and forth hoping that I could fell it without using the blunt saw, a still-whippy branch pronged off her gardening hat. It left her bald and sullen-looking, and I laughed out loud.

'Go back to your bookshop!'

But I didn't, because we picnicked at one o'clock as usual on the stony beach, though at first there was rather a silence until, wheezing a good deal, she uncorked the wine. Then, after a glass, we began to laugh, first about our appearance, for working in the dust had made us like Ayrshire colliers, only she, as I told her, looked more like Othello with her severe nose. Then we laughed about the hat and about her being cross about it. We only stopped when that healing bottle of wine was finished.

When I rowed her home late that afternoon, I'd already begun to feel something new, which was a really tremendous pride in our tidying-up operations. Also, I had caught the faintest whiff of anticipation for a spring not yet here, when we would have planted up those dead islands with trees again.

For this reason, I enjoyed the evenings when rather tipsy we used to go through her plant catalogues. Whether from past habit or present need I don't know, she drank fairly robustly, and so, to be companionable, did I. As a matter of fact drink suited her, because it rounded into gentleness her rather over-emphatic nature, released a latent sympathy and showed her sense of humour and a sort of jolly rakery that began to charm me. Heightened, possibly over-heightened by drink (whisky, brandy, rum—her alarming *saki* I never dared to taste again, though she did), we ransacked the nurserymen's catalogues, and then we'd go walking about in nutteries and spinneys that weren't even there yet, and we'd smell flowers which were still dry seeds in a packet or in peeling bulbs. I have never known anything quite like this before, outside a lover's bed. I mean the expanding of the word, so that it can become an experience. Or conversely, the imploding of the experience so that it becomes a word.

Erigeron 'Dignity', Eriogonum umbellatum, Erodium Macradenum . . . Sometimes she sang these prosy names like a Te Deum. Sometimes to 'Three Blind Mice' or 'The Ashgrove', 'Eryngium, agavifolium alpinium, and bourgatii . . . but the trees,' she said, 'will have to be quick-growing ones or I shan't see them! It's odd to be so old that it's not really worth planting an oak tree, for instance.'

I said I thought this was a bit selfish, and what about her grandchildren. Oaks were always planted for grandchildren.

'I wasn't thinking about grandchildren,' she said. 'I was thinking that you'd see it but I wouldn't.'

'You can't be jealous,' I said, 'at the time I've got left that you've already had?' She smiled and didn't say anything, so I could only assume she was jealous.

'After all, compared with me you've had the best,' I said. 'Listen!' I said. 'You've lived BC, that means before the combustion engine. You've had "hand made", you've had privacy, you've had God! Look what I've got to look forward to!'

'But it's the looking forward that becomes so precious as time runs out!'

'But . . .'

'We'll drink to the present then, the only tense we can't quarrel about, the only tense we really share.'

'Your past,' I said.

'Oceanic past. A seamless world where nothing went wrong, though I expect it did and I've forgotten.'

Her severe black eyes saw it again, the large mill-pond at her home, and chugging across it the steamboat she and her father had just completed, the white smell of its steam mingling oddly with the rather sickly scent of hawthorn on the banks.

'There was a dear old pony called Crim,' she said, 'and Jack the dog, and when my brothers went back to school and father sailed out to Hong Kong, we went everywhere together. I once paddled Jack across the pond in a wooden beer-cooler . . .'

She made me see the lady fern and wild anemones sprouting from the stones which held up the pond banks and, further in, hidden in the screening grass, the dull green twayblades.

'Nothing obliterates first visions. Don't we return to them again and again? In our ends are our beginnings, though I suppose there are always the occasional clouds.'

'What clouds?'

'Well, dreadful dislocations of experience that everyone born under the sun has to go through.'

'You?'

'Not now! Not now! I'd rather concentrate on what we're trying to do.'

I'd drunk too much and longed to go to bed. Her hand, when I took it, was rough as ever, youthful with work, and when I bent to kiss her cheek I saw the deep lines which gave her eyes their expression—all angry lines, and short-sighted lines, considering lines and laughing lines. The cheek below them was soft and firm.

During this time Hugh came frequently, which in its way was a bore, because I wanted to be left alone with my ancient Shafto, free to enjoy her company, and to sound, as far as I dared, her curious deeps.

Hugh's presence didn't really favour this. He was missing Belle passionately, and wouldn't stop telling us so. Even now he was engaging in a tedious interchange of letters in which he was urging Belle, who'd taken a job with Oxfam, to return to him. Belle on her side was being insistent on careful explorations of motive, sieving minutely Hugh's intentions, making assessments of the future prospects of the marriage. Quite right, I suppose. Poor Hugh, bogged down with correspondence, simply missed her dreadfully.

I see now that people, even after their calamity, don't change nearly as much as the novelists would have us believe, which is disappointing. Rather they experience a shift of concentration, of interest. Hugh was now primarily interested in Belle's return, and no longer concerned, since his heady success with the Rococo Symposium, with glamorous aesthetic isolation. He had already been lured twice from his fastness since June to lecture, rather oddly, on aspects of the Neo-Classic. Rosa, it appeared, had heartily approved of this, which was stranger still, but then her concentration of interest had also shifted, Hugh told us, from guardianship of the 'flame' to the rude theological student with whom she was apparently still having an affair.

'In the end I'm afraid it all comes down to sex,' Hugh said. 'One hopes of course that it's an enlargement of character, but I'm afraid that it's nearly always what's below the navel that rules us.'

'Are you serious?' asked Mrs Shafto.

'Well, it's kinder isn't it?' said Hugh. 'The old belly. In the end I prefer the dear old belly.'

'What a change,' I said, 'remembering all those lashings and kickings of your outraged sensibility!'

'Ah well, beggars mayn't be choosers,' he replied comfortably. He had just had good news from Belle. She was winding up the Oxfam job and would be home in ten days.

'You're sure it won't embarrass you if I'm still here?'

'Good God, no! I should have thought we'd all been so bleached and scoured by what we'd been through that there wouldn't be one drop of animosity left in any of us. All we care for now surely is the quiet life!'

My life was quiet. Never more quiet. To the fury of my assistant I let the business of the shop go hang, though I did remove the cat and most of my bookbinding gear down to Kate Shafto's workshop. Here, as the summer nights began to draw in we'd gravely, in an aroma of boiling glue and sawn wood, set to work. She'd laid down the keel of a new boat, a brigantine this time; her beautiful and meticulous working drawings were already pinned to the walls, the elegant snout of the model caught in a vice, the dowelled frames ready to go in. She'd whistle like a groom when she worked and then she'd stop, poised like a snooker player, one eye closed, judging lines I imagine, then back she'd go to neatly tapping and gluing and whistling, while I absently folded and refolded paper.

'It was India that dislocated me,' she said suddenly one evening, straightening up from her boat. 'My marriage in India! It was like being ripped from my element, can you possibly understand? Like a terribly powerful recreation of oneself.'

She saw, again, herself and Rory lying on the bed surveying her body torn open, betrayed, but over which they rejoiced nevertheless, as at the fall of a city.

'Jaipur! Srinagar! Rawalpindi!' she cried, furiously buzzing her small hand-drill. 'So beautiful, and oh such a waste! But it was too late. I'd been turned to stone.'

'What do you mean?'

'I've often asked myself what the meaning is of those stories in Ovid about Diana and her followers,' she said, not taking any notice. 'I mean those curious girls who never wanted to marry anyone, but who wanted, as I did, with Jack and Crim, to go wandering all day alone in the woods. Daphne and Syrinx for instance: do you think they were simply neurotic girls who were turned into trees and reeds just to keep them quiet, or were they really priestesses?'

'Priestesses?'

'Of Nature. It's men who call you forth from that. From that dreamless chastity, just as the father, when he impregnates the mother, makes from her a new and separate creature,' continued Kate Shafto resuming her delicate light tappings of the wooden dowels. 'Don't you think that the Fall is such a witty masculine version of the truth? Woman was there first, of course, we know that, and then, into her untidy, dreamy, overgrown garden which was at once so earthly and so spiritual, came a man; the alienator, the separator, the subcreator, the lawgiver. The only true part of the myth,' laughed Kate Shafto, 'is the snake!'

'What has this got to do with India?'

'India!' she said. 'Now just that word, like the word "Africa" must mean to some other people. How can I tell you?' The room grew still but for the sound of the glue bubbling. 'How can I evoke for you those fierce beakie-looking warrior princesses? There was even a harsh civetty smell from the folds of their clothes when they moved. God knows, the men must have been cruel if the women were like that. So secret, cruel, strong, proud. I was told that they were descendants of the Jains. And the cattle moved slow and white as great moons, their enormous brown eyes encircled with kohl, made huger by the flies which clustered like thick black raisins. I remember there were funny dipping birds that left their drying claw-marks in water on the temple steps. That was at Khajuraho, where there are figures of lovers everywhere. Such soft, sweet lovers! Yet the young man's eyes soft as doe's eyes had eyebrows above them like curved daggers, and although he fondled his mistress's breasts so tenderly his mouth was curly and arrogant. They were both laughing. It was unforgettable. Cruel and sweet. And lumbering across this, across the little dipping bird and the white oxen and the lovers were the English with their silly fox terriers all called Fly and Dash and Slipper, and their punts. Yes, punts. And in the enormous heat, uniforms. Like machines of order!'

She moved her cheek from the twisted gold captain's insignia on his shoulder, and longing for the softness of his skin gently undid the buttons of his tunic thinking not at all of the mess dance but of the bird prints drying on the stone of that empyrean of gentle lovers seen for the first time this morning. She couldn't get it out of her mind. The smiling mouths met, the slanted half-shut eyes, the soft hands felt gently for the warm fruit growing below the neat wasp waists. Absently now she sought to divest him of this ridiculous husk of stuff and braid, her fingers tripping over the tight buttoned waistband of his mess trousers.

'I say,' he said laughing with embarrassment. 'Steady on!'

The mess trousers were so tight-fitting that they could only be pulled on if the batman had first rolled them down over the shining mess pumps into which he stepped, rolling and smoothing the trousers up and over calves, thighs, bottom. They could only be removed by a reverse procedure.

Briskly he began undoing his own flies. She, having wanted him naked, so that she might engulf him like a soft devouring flower, began to laugh.

'I'm simply not going to take off my trousers,' he said.

They made love effectively enough in spite of various tapes and buttons.

There had been something curiously mechanical about the whole business, some quality that had put her in mind of the dreadful image, often so much admired, of Wellington pleasuring his wife nine times with his boots on. Or was it Marlborough? Anyway, like some terrible piston. She had conceived Hugh, but it had not been what she wanted.

He was a kind man, and when he saw her distress he was himself dismayed and tried on subsequent occasions to please her, for he was not inexperienced with women like so many of them were. He tried things that other women had taught him and that he'd read in books, for he was neither narrow-minded nor a prude, and he loved her. Something, however, seemed to have been lost, something of which she had known the value and he had not. Even after any particular effort on his part had made her desire to laugh, for she hadn't wanted what had been taught by other women, nor had she wanted the wisdom of the Kama Sutra, the screeching and pummelling and slapping had seemed contrived in the extreme. However, she never laughed at him. She was fond of him and didn't want to hurt him, nor for him to know that after that night, wanting the best, and knowing certainly that she'd never have it with him, she had privately and very decorously given up.

In the end they settled for a sort of school pals' union in which, growing humorous and a little hard, she succumbed to the prevalent fashion of Eton bobs and flat breasts (learning to shoot and play golf and polo) and this, stirring some latent and innocent homosexuality in him, excited him sufficiently for them to be tolerably happy.

'But in a kind of terrible sexual jealousy I began to persecute the natural world,' explained Kate Shafto. 'Shooting especially. I grew to adore shooting. Tiger shooting. I wore, of course you'll laugh to see me now, but I was slim then, I even wore tiger. And I turned my eyes away from all the lovely little brown babies and their gentle mamas and papas, and from all the birds and the beggars and the sacred white cows, because, for a time, I needed to turn my eyes away. And then one leave we went back to the Khajuraho temples, and this time I was glad to find that the feeling I'd had there was dead. Quite dead. And when, in a kind of ritual, Rory and I slept together afterwards, we both laughed like mad at the memory of that first time. A kind of veil had come over it, and I couldn't understand what I had seen in it any more.

'I suppose after that in some ways I became a kind of imitation man,' said Kate Shafto, cheerfully stirring the appalling fish glue. 'I divided, as men do, everything into black and white, good and bad, body and soul. I've asked myself since, has there ever been the authentic woman's voice in the world? I have only been able to think of Sappho, or of that Greek pot in the B.M. with the Eumenides as wasps stinging a lot of men in troublesome places . . . I always like to think that a woman potter did that. Oh, the too-vaunted Greeks. Do you remember the horror of that barbarous Periclean funeral oration that everyone even now goes on about? So cruel, so cruel, not a woman's voice to be heard in all that catalogue of slaughter.'

'When did you begin thinking like this?'

'As I grew wiser, I like to think; or was it just when sex began growing less important? It's so confusing, isn't it? I mean it's so hard to tell whether wisdom is really wisdom or merely the desires of the flesh subsiding?' She laughed, a deep wheezing laugh that ended in a coughing fit.

'Did you ever rediscover what you saw at the Khajuraho temples?' I asked her.

'No. Never that. But when at last we came home I began gardening. At first it was the kind of gardening that most people do. Treating the garden as a kind of tiresome junk room that's got to be swept out from time to time. And then, as I watched the plants growing, I began to remember things I'd forgotten. I also began to see the deadly criminal waste, it's commonplace now, but it wasn't then, that unlike in heaven, nature here on earth is expendable as is all love and beauty and peace.'

'I wish I'd been here!' I said.

'Do you?' She looked up for a moment from the wooden dowels she was deftly tapping in. 'It makes me feel curiously happy to talk to you about it.'

Belle came back. I hardly noticed, wouldn't have known, except that Hugh didn't come for about ten days or so. When they did call in Belle, naturally perhaps, seemed a bit wary of me, but she needn't have been. I was too absorbed.

One night when Kate Shafto'd stopped planking her ship for a moment, and was fussing about making Nescafé, I read her Rochester's poem, partly to tease her:

> Ancient person for whom I
> All the flattering youth defy
> Long be it ere thou grow old
> Aching shaking crazy cold
> But still continue as thou art,
> Ancient person of my heart.

'I'm glad you didn't read any further,' she said laughing, 'the concluding verse gets so very unseemly.' And then she asked, 'How much longer do you think we can go on like this?'

'Why not for ever?'

'No, perhaps it is a stupid question. You don't think, do you, that the disparity in our ages makes it "unseemly"?'

'Unseemly? How could it be unseemly? I'm happy.'

'And I'm happy.'

But I'm afraid Belle and Hugh thought it was unseemly.

'You ought to go and see someone who could help you, Hero, you really ought to. I should have thought that you'd have learnt something about yourself by now. It's really so very, very neurotic attaching yourself to one person after another. It isn't adult of you, you know.'

That was Belle, and I probably only imagined that she sounded slightly aggrieved when she said it. She and Hugh seemed quite happy again. Even if they weren't, they had begun to be tyrannous in the way they tried to mould everyone else to what they thought they ought to be. In the end they nagged so much that Kate Shafto got tired of it and said she was going off on tour until the trees she'd ordered came from the nursery.

'Well, unseemly or not, here I am!' I said as we came out of the Beaudesert gates. She smiled and hit the kerb. In spite of being taught by Sir Malcolm Campbell, she was a frightful driver, seeing too intensely, I think, as she sped along. It reminded me of what Charlotte Brontë had said about Emily, how for her, 'flowers brighter than the rose bloomed in the blackest of the wild heath, how out of a sullen hollow in a livid hillside, her mind could make an Eden'. I asked Kate Shafto whether she was secretly replanting brakes and diverting water-courses as we motored along, and she said actually yes, so after that I drove.

Twice the old Riley broke down, once in North Wales on that unfriendly tundra-like stretch just before you come to the Horse Shoe Pass. Another time the fanbelt went at nightfall just outside horrible Bodnant. It didn't matter. Nothing does, I find, if you are enjoying positively every moment you spend with someone.

After ten days we turned for home, not because we were tired of each other's company, but because we wanted to see what was happening on the islands, and anyway we wanted to get back to our evenings making boats and bookbinding.

It was on the way back that I took the only photograph of her that I ever did take, standing beside the large urn of pink granite in Llantysilio churchyard.

'With a squeeze even you could fit into it, darling!' I said, and because it was so funny I photographed her beside it, just like that, leaning on her walking-stick.

It was stupid though. Because taking the photograph marked the moment, I kept thinking about death all the way back. It is the big hazard when you love someone so much older than yourself. It takes the place of fear of unfaithfulness when you are young. But it was eventually driven out of my head by the time we got home because we found that at last the trees had come.

TWELVE

When we got back we planted trees solidly for five days on end. We began early in the morning when the water in the gravel pit was a shield of black glass, sealed off by mist from the September sky in which the sun shone and starlings were chattering. On the sixth day Kate Shafto went up to Town and I continued planting on my own.

I noticed, rowing over, that among the trees so neatly stitched in sacking were not only the larches and quick-growing poplars that we'd agreed on, but some young oaks too, and I took this as a kind of tacit compliment and was touched.

It felt odd to be without her even for a day. I missed her ramming down the earth with the heels of her old Newmarket boots and numbly joining the wire anti-rabbit collars around the specimen trees, or impatiently tumbling out the contents of the named bags of crocus and snowdrop and anemone. I missed her particularly at the lunch break when we used to talk about what it was going to be like next spring when the cherries would flower and the little beech-trees come into leaf.

I sat alone wolfing sandwiches at the water's edge and tried to bring into perspective the odd, and what some people would certainly have called arrested, sort of life I was now leading. They would have been curious, possibly, to learn how total the arrest was. Not only of career, of emotion, in a way of time, but of my body also. Whether owing to some side-kick of Phage 34 or to strains of one kind or another, my curse had stopped. It seemed symbolic. Then, as the last of the mist melted from the now radiant water I pondered my friendship with Kate Shafto. It seemed that no present-day categories existed for it; they are hopelessly narrow in any case. I remembered Belle speaking long ago of lost dimensions of relationship, and it seemed that it might be one of these, for it was not precisely a mother and daughter relationship, nor yet one of elder and younger sister. It seemed, as I thought about it, to be something rather more like the relation of acolyte to priestess. That situation would have come near to the feeling of complicity and love I felt for her. It was an affection hard to describe, for it had about it the curious touch of passion once shared, though at a very long time back in the past, in the blood almost: and of a passion, or perhaps even an ecstasy, which was due to be shared at some great distance in the future. Yet these perceptions of past and future time seemed to be contained completely in the quiet almost humdrum present in which we lived together.

By evening all was altered.

I worked hard all that afternoon, and in fact I completed the planting of one entire island. I did exactly as she'd shown me, as she'd drawn beforehand in the dust with a stick in a paisley-like pattern of walks and tree glades. Into this dusty map I dug wild cherry and ash and hazel, and where there were gaps I threw handfuls of daffodils and bluebells, planting them where they fell for the sake of naturalness. I didn't bother to put anti-rabbit collars round the trees because I really couldn't believe that any rabbit would be able to swim so far and I was eager to please her by getting as much done as I could.

By teatime when I'd finished I could see, looking over the water, that she'd got home, because the old Riley was in the drive. She hadn't called out for me to come over to fetch her to see the works or anything; she'd just gone straight into the house. When I'd tied up the boat I went indoors and found her standing at the drawing-room window. She was just lighting a cigarette.

'What about coming to look at all the hard work I've done?'

'Don't be so impatient. I was just about to!'

'Nice day then?' I asked, and then, 'What's the matter?'

She turned round and said, 'Apparently I've got a small growth on one of my vocal chords. At the moment the man's not sure whether it's cancer or not.'

So that was her lovely rough voice that was so funny and sounded like Hutch when she sang.

'I thought it had always been hoarse?'

'Yes I think it has, but perhaps not quite so hoarse as it is now.'

She took my arm and we walked slowly out of the front door and down to the water's edge.

'How well you've done, little one; I can see from here.'

'You know that it can be a tremendously successful operation,' I was saying. 'There's that actor, I've forgotten his name. Well, he's still about, and I once knew a doctor who had it . . . and oh darling, why didn't you tell me you were going and I'd have come with you. I'd have wanted to!'

'It may well not be malignant after all, but he says there's a lump of some kind, so he wants me to go in for a night next week to snip a bit off and have it sent to the path. lab. It probably isn't anything at all, like the Phage 34, remember?' And she squeezed my arm.

In the night I couldn't sleep, and going back to my room from the bathroom I passed her door and saw that her light was on. When I went in she was sitting up in bed and was either drawing or making notes in a small sketch-book. She laid it carefully to one side and didn't say anything, but she held out her hand and I went over to her. Her rough, thin, warm hand. I let it go and lay down beside her and put my arms round her. Neither of us said anything for a time.

'I closed the curtains in case the light attracted mosquitoes,' she said at last, 'but there's such a lovely moon. Pull them back and turn off the light!'

I drew the curtains and there was a huge moon like a yellow fruit, and in its soft light the islands with their newly-planted trees looked like furred animals. Asleep.

I turned back and got into the place she'd made for me beside her in the great bed. Its sheets and pillows smelt of the burnt orange scent of Portugal water which she used instead of cologne or lavender, and I lay on, quiet, beside her fat, cool, bulk, watching the water reflecting over the ceiling like quivering wire.

'You do know that I'll live it with you, every moment of it, if this is to be your death,' I said.

'Ssh, romantic one. I know you would, but it's not really very likely. Let's just be peaceful. Look at the moon!'

I watched it as it moved, now pear-, now apple-shaped, through the uneven bottle-glass of the windows and then, in spite of misery, I fell asleep.

She allowed me to drive her up to London, and I stayed with a schoolfriend while she went into the home. She was allowed out after forty-eight hours, during which she'd teased and terrorised the nurses into hysterics, and I drove her back.

Five days later we got the all clear as far as the cancer was concerned, though they were still undecided about the surgery.

I wanted her to have a celebration then and to ask Hugh and Belle to it, but she wouldn't, and in the end I was glad because it meant that we could get back all the sooner to our routine, she working on her boat and I binding whatever it was. Actually I remember what it was quite well because it never got finished. It was *Gil Blas*. We did this at night, and in the daytime we finished the whole of the planting, down to the last tree stake, the last peeling bulb. When we'd finished she opened a bottle of Riesling and we drank half of it and the rest we poured out as a libation. She chose Ceres, which I suppose was quite appropriate. I, after a great deal of hesitation, because I always fear the wrath of neglected gods when it comes to libations, chose, as usual, Apollo. Then for a time we walked round our immature woods.

'Do you think Zeus felt like this when he restored the world after Deucalion's blood?' I said he thought they must have.

Then we took to the boat, and looked at our handiwork from the water, I rowing her from one island to another, and it really did seem quite wonderful that those plumey patterns we'd drawn in the ash had already expanded into trees that would branch and leaf and beneath whose shade one day sheep would crowd, as it says in the song.

Yet I was anxious. Still anxious in spite of the cancer test being negative, still hopelessly, so mortally afraid of losing her. I tried various means for getting what I wanted. Excuses and deceits. In the end, indulgent, as though with some slightly annoying child, she gave in, and I moved my bed in beside her and we slept in the same room. But although we could now, lying horizontal, which after all is the most comfortable position in the world, talk about anything, or laugh, or just lie dozing as lovers will at that most beautiful time in life, which is after passion is slaked (which I suppose was really the moon of my life with her), I don't think she really liked me being in her room. An intrusion of privacy perhaps, *lèse-majesté* of some kind, I don't know, but I also didn't care, for at least with her hardly ever out of my sight I could pretend not to be so anxious as I really was.

Yet perhaps after all I communicated it to her, for at the beginning of October, when we were still waiting for the surgeon's decision, she escaped.

I'd been over to the shop. I'd let my flat long ago. Understandably the assistant, in a burst of exasperation, had given notice. I spent an unwilling day there going through what was left of the stock and trying to decide what to do with it. When I got back in the evening she'd gone.

She'd left no address. 'Darling,' she wrote in a note of which the rest is too private and sad to give here, 'there were other warnings. Contact Hugh McLean and he'll explain the whole thing to you . . .'

Her precious body was washed up ten days later on the rocks off Skomer where we'd been not so long before. On our jaunt. It was by then a thing. A blown nibbled bag, caught just at the moment before it was due to disintegrate into something else, which in time would become a fish perhaps, a bird, coral, weed. I went to identify it with Hugh, and was only able to by the signet ring embedded in her icy black finger.

It was a paradisial day, the smoky violet rocks running out into a sea as blue and rare as the Adriatic, and from inaccessible nursery caves, filled rapturously by the sea, you could hear the petulant moaning of seal pups. I walked on my own towards Strumble Head and had my sandwiches out of the wind in a turf dip behind a great rock that was a garden of coloured stonecrops and lichens. Afterwards I went to the cliff edge and looked over. Nothing. Only stones green and stippled with brown dye like gulls' eggs. And then, after a time, I saw the stones move, and it was a waking seal, then three seals; a bluish looking male and two females. I think it was a conversation piece; all three creatures were lolling on the rocks snorting and sneezing, and there was an apparently untouched fish (an engagement present?) lying on the rock beside them. I was afraid they might see me, so I left them for a while, and then, when I returned, it was as I had thought, and two of the seals were lying united, the male holding the female in his flippers and they were drifting gently back and forth in the clear shallows as the current took them, softly eddying, the tide washing over them. When I returned a third time there had been some kind of quarrel, due, no doubt, to the presence of the other mistress. The lovers had parted. I heard a great deal of sneezing and snorting and complaining, and the male was chasing one of the females below the water. From where I stood I could see their underwater movement braiding the surface in a perpetually snaking infinity sign, like this ∞.

I could imagine it all too well. Given time she would sink quite easily a bottle of whisky or brandy. In any case, to prove it, alcohol in gross excess was found in her stomach. The low-slung smoky moon which had shone that first night when I thought I'd lost her but hadn't, had come round again. It would have been a high sea, with the seals, as they do in the moonlight, circling offshore from their caves. It wasn't difficult to imagine . . . sometimes there are stranded seal pups waiting for the incoming tide to lap them off the stones and into their element again. If there'd been such a pup she would have waited I think for that sublime moment when the water comes up to the flippers, to the downy white breast, to the eager butterfly nostrils. Then the seal, which is such a poor hobbledehoy sort of creature on land, is changed by water at this moment into another creature, the clumsy body becoming, in the familiar element, new and glorious, plunging, rolling, curveting out from Port Stinion and into the St George's Channel and then, moonlight guttering ecstatically in the submerged eyes, out and out towards the Atlantic.

I was desperate with grief and anger, for whatever it was going to be, I had wanted to live her death with her. And she had cheated me of what seemed the greatest gift she could make me, my chance to love her, no matter how poor, mad, terrible. It wouldn't have mattered.

Besides, leaving myself out of it, the greatest authorities abhorred what she'd done. 'There is a doctrine whispered in secret,' Plato had written to confound this action of hers, 'that man (and so presumably woman too) is a prisoner who has no right to open the door and run away.' Even I could have added his comment, 'this is a great mystery which I do not quite understand'.

Sometimes, weeding or planting her garden afterwards, magnificent diapasons of hatred would boom in my head. Sometimes it was quite the opposite, and instead there were Te Deums of love and gratitude. Words reverberating from the Sacrament, 'All this in Memory of you! All this! All this!'

I can't write poetry, so I clutched shamelessly at other people's, poetry seeming to be the only language in which to think of her, in which to express my grief.

> Hard for your pupil lover, who can match
> No living lustre with your swaddled face
> I had not guessed that my poor eyes must watch
> So long to find you at the dancing place.

I would remember something that couldn't afterwards be found in Donne; that perhaps too clever idea that Love recalls Death, and Death, as on that hot October afternoon when Hugh and I had identified her body, Love. And I also remembered how Donne had said that each lover's soul is the body of the other. It was an idea that I'd had no time to tell her, but which would have expressed perfectly our reconciliation, which was of age and time and temperament and heart. Oh, everything.

Yet reconciliation is, I suppose, only a truce. There is on this earth no painless formula for commuting that constant revolution which is life, that terrible restripping, renewing, re-seeking, again and again and again and again.

By her action she had removed our affection out of the structures of time that were familiar to me, leaving, for her own purpose, our adventure—unfinished.

'Now,' she had said, 'do without me!'

McNally Editions reissues books that are not widely known but have stood the test of time, that remain as singular and engaging as when they were written. Available in the US wherever books are sold or by subscription from mcnallyeditions.com.

1. Han Suyin, *Winter Love*
2. Penelope Mortimer, *Daddy's Gone A-Hunting*
3. David Foster Wallace, *Something to Do with Paying Attention*
4. Kay Dick, *They*
5. Margaret Kennedy, *Troy Chimneys*
6. Roy Heath, *The Murderer*
7. Manuel Puig, *Betrayed by Rita Hayworth*
8. Maxine Clair, *Rattlebone*
9. Akhil Sharma, *An Obedient Father*
10. Gavin Lambert, *The Goodby People*
11. Wyatt Harlan, *Elbowing the Seducer*
12. Lion Feuchtwanger, *The Oppermanns*
13. Gary Indiana, *Rent Boy*
14. Alston Anderson, *Lover Man*
15. Michael Clune, *White Out*
16. Martha Dickinson Bianchi, *Emily Dickinson Face to Face*
17. Ursula Parrott, *Ex-Wife*
18. Margaret Kennedy, *The Feast*
19. Henry Bean, *The Nenoquich*
20. Mary Gaitskill, *The Devil's Treasure*
21. Elizabeth Mavor, *A Green Equinox*
22. Dinah Brooke, *Lord Jim at Home*
23. Phyllis Paul, *Twice Lost*
24. John Bowen, *The Girls*